TO ENVY THE BIRDS

K.C. MENDOZA

Ebook ISBN: 978-1-7377459-1-4

Print ISBN: 978-1-7377459-0-7

A special thanks to my friend, Sara (Instagram @saraayalaart) for helping, giving advice and giving me inspiration to complete part 2 and 3 of this trilogy. Truly grateful from the bottom of my heart.

Table of Content

This book is dedicated to the person who taught me about love and pain, simultaneously, at the same time.

CHAPTER 1

I'm blinded by the sun gleaming off my windshield. The light hits directly into my eyes and it causes me to lose focus, so I cover them by lifting my palm against the sunshine. My head hurts. Sleep deprivation does that. I stare at the road as I drive through the empty highway, not looking anywhere but ahead of me. Stockton sure looks deteriorated.

It's been weeks since I've driven at this time, almost outside of curfew time, of course. The sunset spreads throughout, and its colors remind me of serenity and warmth, nothing to do with how I feel right now.

All I can think of is Carol. I must find her.

She's been missing for days now.

I drive into French Camp Road and to the convenience store at the corner, a few blocks away from my house. A gut-wrenching feeling settles as I find myself breaking the one rule my dad hammered unto us ever since we were young:

Be home no later than six.

The time is 6:15 pm but I pull the keys from the ignition anyway. My heart is pounding, and I find it hard to breathe. The day is getting darker, so it makes me even more anxious. I push the front door open, and a man stops me midway, placing his hand at the edge of the handle. "Sorry, we are closed now." He says as he attempts to pull the door from my grip. "I won't be long, I promise," I say. He remains silent, looking behind me to see if I came with anyone. Once he realizes I am alone, he allows me to enter but not without shaking his head. A shake that assures me that he is bothered by my presence.

I look towards the back counter and begin walking towards it. The man walks behind me, following me, "What do you need?" He asks, somewhat disturbed. "I need to see your electronics," I say. He remains silent for a moment but points behind me without saying another word.

I feel a rush of guilt for being such a pain in the ass. I hear him mumble something to a woman, but I pretend not to listen. He goes behind the counter and crosses his arms, "What do you need? Hurry," he says. I pull out a cord and hand it to him. "I need to plug this in. You guys have public sockets here, right?" I ask as I hear the woman sigh loudly behind me.

He turns around, plugs it, and hands me the end of it. With slight hesitation, I pull a cellphone out of my purse and connect it. Pressing the button was a worse idea. The cellphone vibrates, and we stare at each other in suspense.

Then, the phone lights up.

Flickering lights surround its case, and within seconds, it begins beeping. I panic and frantically start pushing buttons, hoping that one of them would shut it off but I hear them screaming at me. The man pushes my hand away, unplugs the cord and tosses it over the countertop. "Get out of here with that thing!" he shouts. Frantic, I drop it inside my purse, but it falls on the floor instead. "I'm sorry, I don't know much of these things!" I shout.

I grab the cord and put it in my bag as I drop to the floor to pick up the cellphone. "You need to get out of here!" The woman yells from the front of the store.

We hear a truck screech outside within a few minutes. "Close it!" The woman shouts as the man rushes to the front of the store. I see her putting money inside a bag and as I see her doing that, I stick my purse in the middle of the counter, right next to the wall.

Three men with masks rush out of a black truck

and towards us—my stomach drops. I can't do much because I am frozen. Praying that the door would be closed by the time they reach us, but when the man pulls out his keys, he is too late. One of the masked men lifts his foot, kicks the door open, and grabs him. The woman screams, and both of them struggle.

I throw myself down to the floor as a gun comes out. They are already inside. I slam my back against the counter, looking for a way out but there is none.

The woman drops the bag with money towards them, and I place my face entirely on the ground. I see the woman putting her face on the floor through the bottom of the counter, but then she turns, and we see each other.

And I can't do anything for her.

I try to move but my face is bolted to the bottom. I stare at her lips as they tremble, and I see the footsteps of one of them approaching her. Then, a scream, as he lifts her.

"Where is she?" He shouts.

I shut my eyes.

"I don't know what you're talking about!"

I look over. The man I was talking to rushes from the floor and begins crawling towards me. He then stumbles up, slams against an aisle, and starts running towards the back. I stare at him as he runs past me and into the back room. The door shuts as I suddenly turn my head back towards the front end of the store, and one of them yells. "There is someone back there!" another shouts, and I turn and see them pointing at me.

Frozen no longer.

My body is exploding internally, screaming to run away, to dissipate. But instead, I slam into the back counter again.

"Get up!" A guy yells as he pulls me. I scream as I lift myself, trying to loosen his grip on my shoulder but when he locks eyes with me, his eyes widen, and his grip loosens.

Another guy walks to us and notices something, "Jack, you're alright?" He asks while he pulls him by the shoulder.

Jack shakes his head. "Yeah, I'm fine," he says.

And just like that. Everything is calm—no more screams, shouts, or struggles.

"Nothing here, Jack…." The third guy joins us, and I'm confused. They walk back but Jack points at me. "Let's take that girl," he says as he starts to walk back towards the front. "What?" Jack stops midway, cocks his two fingers towards me, and says, "Eric, we're taking that one…." He makes a face; the unsettling look creeps around his eyes as they open wide, but he listens, nonetheless. "Come on," he says.

"What? No!" I scream.

He lifts his hands to show me he means no harm, but I know better! And as I try to pull away, he keeps telling me that they are only asking me questions. His hand caves under my arm and I swing it away. Struggling but I can't free myself. They are taking me!

The woman is still on the floor, and I hear a silent prayer. I assume it is for me. "Please!" I pull away as I see we are approaching their truck. I pull myself towards my car, but he is too strong, and I am losing this battle.

"No! Please!" I scream as Eric struggles.

My body slams on the side of the truck as I beg for them to let me go. "We'll let you go right now," he assures me but Jack walks outside a few moments later and he walks around the front of the truck and towards the driver's seat, "Hey Jack, what do we need to ask?" He begins as Jack opens the driver's door.

"We're taking this one to the house," he says as he jumps in and shuts the door.

"No!" I launch myself towards the store, but Eric grabs me.

"I don't have money! Please!"

"What are you talking about, Jack?"

"Get her in the car, Eric!"

Eric turns to look inside the store and then back

at me. Confused. He doesn't know why Jack wants to take me, which is even more unsettling.

I pull at his hand and drop on the floor. I attempt once again to crawl away, but he grabs me. The truck door opens, and I stare at that void—the black hole. I am for sure dead.

Eric places me in between him and the truck. "Please!" I cry as he begins pushing me inside. "Please… my parents are waiting for me! We have a curfew! I need to be home!" Eric tugs on my hand as the third guy helps and they push me inside the car.

"Jack, we are not…."

"Get in!" Jack shouts.

Eric rushes to the other side and pulls me. I hit them, trying to free myself from their grip but as Eric yells, "Close it," the third guy shuts the door. And then, I hear metal clinking together.

Eric removes his gun, places it on the seat, and I stop. Back to frozen. Back to feeling numbed. Looking at the gun without blinking. All my energy is wasted by staring at this gun. Even if we were driving away, that matters more to me right now.

Jack is mumbling something, but the wind is making it hard for me to hear. And as Jack and the other guy talk, Eric leans in, "I'll help you out, just cooperate for now," He whispers, but I back away. He leans back into the seat—a worried look. His fingers are fidgeting, and he stares up and glances at me every couple of seconds. He runs his hands up and down, adjusting his mask. I should be more concerned now that he is too.

Reality hits me as my parents and my life are left back there inside the store. I left it all. Not knowing if I am going to return. Holding in tears, a heavy feeling sets in the middle of my chest.

"I have no idea!" The third guy shouts. "It has to be in Sacramento. That was the last time we heard anything," He screams into a cellphone.

And Jack is quiet, staring at the road. "I just hope we find something soon," Eric says.

"Jack, we have to try Sacramento again!"

"Jay, shut up! We were there this afternoon!" Eric yells back. And Jack?

Nothing.

He glances up at me through the rearview mirror, and then looks back at the road. I keep my chin low but raise my eyes to look at him. If they are not kidnappers, then why am I here? Why is he looking at me that way? I lean to the right so that Jack doesn't look at me that way anymore. I can't. He is terrifying.

I look out and see that the night is here. I look ahead to where the 5 freeway and 580 junction meet. And when we drive through the highway division, they pull their masks off. They are younger than expected and not as I imagined them to be.

So normal.

They don't look like criminals. They don't have those face tattoos that my dad used to talk about. They weren't from another country like my grandpa used to say. They looked like everyone else, and they didn't have an accent either.

They are American, just like me.

Jay, with black hair and thick eyebrows, looks the most normal. He has no tattoos, no piercings, and looks like a kid. Eric has red wavy hair with a chain lock beard, blue eyes, and freckles. And Jack has brown hair, about four inches at the top with shaved sides. His hair is combed back over his head, and he is muscular but skinny. Several tattoos cover his arms and fingers, and a full beard covers his mouth and chin.

But Jack. He looks furious. Like he is going to hurt me as soon as he gets a chance. That's the look he's giving me.

"Please," I choke.

"Stop," Jack interrupts. "You beg once more, and you'll leave me no choice but to leave your body in a ditch."

CHAPTER 2

I should have listened to my parents. They now wasted most of their lives trying to protect us from danger, but we didn't listen. I was doing exactly what my parents told Carol not to do. I was walking right under her footsteps.

And now, look at me.

This is where I am, just as Carol might be.

My mom is probably screaming at my dad to go out and look for us. But my dad is standing by the door, staring at the darkness; a darkness he is afraid of.

My mom's screams shatter my brain, and their arguments are loud in my head. Who's to blame for our wrongdoing?

I hear them.

What did they do wrong in raising us?

Mom, Dad, I am here. Trapped.

I wish they could hear me; just to tell them a simple I love you. At least to say goodbye, hug them, and ask them to find Carol instead.

My mom had faith in me. "Go find Carol," she said. "But during the day, Kate. Only during the day,"

And I failed. I am such an idiot!

I can't believe I am putting her in this place again. I sent her back in the past to the day she nearly lost both of us, the "Better Life Movement" of Stockton.

A great decision by the city of Sacramento.

Not so great in the end.

During the downfall of the American government, crime rates spiked at a frightening rate. Parents planned to evacuate and move to Europe because Europe was the best place to be.

But families couldn't leave together. That would cause too much attention and the government surely wouldn't allow it, so they got together and decided to send the children away first with a couple of trusted adults. The decision was secretly made in our Sacramento church, and they had agreed.

The date was November 26, 2049.

A bus was scheduled for San Francisco. This bus, arranged to pick up fifty children, would take us to a childcare center built for us in Europe.

It was simple, they said. Two adults had connections with European refugee camps. They would give us food and shelter for six months right about when another group of adults would meet us.

The church had finalized the details just a week before. "They will be protected; they will be taken care of. This guarantees them a better life. Better than here. This is no future for children," they said.

My mom described it as the "Sea of Tears" because she said she remembers the sound of crying swimming throughout our church. Moms and dads hugging their children would cry in silence, others would scream at eachother , some said nothing at all.

Many of them knew that leaving the city would be a problem, so they would never get to see their children anymore. But Europe was the way to go.

"Their hands, they shook as I handed them their care packages," mom said. "The tears falling on their sign-up sheets broke my heart," she added.

And as dad had a final meeting with the directors, mom had decided all by herself what fate Carol and I would have.

She stepped out of the church as everyone was getting their final instructions.

She had decided that Carol and I would stay.

"Why isn't Carol and Kate here?" Dad said as

Mom turned away from him. "Cristina!" he shouted. "Why aren't Kate and Carol here?" Dad was waving the release form in her face, but Mom snatched the paper away,

"They're not going!" She yelled.

"They can't stay here. They have to go! We collectively decided it was best for the children!"

"Why do they have to go, Andrew!? They have been fine with us, here at home!"

"This isn't a home for them!"

"We will never leave their side!"

"That is beside the point!"

"They're staying!"

"No, they're not!"

"Andrew, our girls. Gone!"

"I understand, honey, but think of their safety,"

"Andrew…"

"Enough! They are going because we care for them!"

And that was it, mom said. She didn't say another word.

The night before the trip, dad walked inside the house with two brown bags. My mom stood up and walked to the back room. I was sitting with Carol in the kitchen. I knew I was leaving, but I didn't understand why just yet.

"Cristina," My dad called softly.

No answer.

And through closed doors, I heard arguing. It was a distant, back and forth. And then, I heard mom cry. Suddenly, the room went quiet. The door slammed open, and my mom ran down the hallway and dropped in front of us. She pulled Carol and me for a hug. She held us tight, and all I can remember was asking myself why she was crying.

Dad walked behind us, kneeled, and placed his hands around mom, and for a long time, I remember the silence.

I guess there was nothing left to be said.

And then dad explained.

We will be going to school abroad. He said that we would learn new things and new ways of life. He told us that we would be protected and be provided shelter until they got there. "Even if mom and dad take longer to get to you, someone will take care of you. Europe is your future."

"Daddy, why aren't you going now?" I remember asking. His eyes became glossy, and he looked away for a second. Dad never cries, I thought.

"Not yet honey. We will get there, but not yet."

In the morning, mom was packing lunch. Carol and I were sitting in the kitchen eating breakfast. I stared at my mom's hands shaking as she placed an apple inside a lunch bag. She grabbed our backpacks and put them in the corner when we heard a scream outside.

"Cristina!" Shouted the neighbor. "Cristina! The bus!"

"What?" Mom screamed back.

"What about the bus? What is going on?" My dad shouted.

"It's been captured! It got stopped coming into Stockton!" The neighbor screamed.

"Lock your doors, don't answer to anyone!" Dad said. The neighbor ran to her house, and dad locked the front and back doors.

This was the first time I saw his shotgun. He pulled it from the closet and told us to go into the back room. "Come on," he said as we followed him.

Dad boarded up the bedroom door, and mom sat Carol and me inside the closet. Mom came inside the closet with us as we heard a knock, and she closed the door.

Another knock, a louder one, startled me, and mom smiled. She lifted her finger to her mouth and closed her eyes.

Another knock. Dad locked the closet from the outside, and mom held Carol and me close to her chest.

Every knock became louder, and mom whispered, "Listen to my heartbeat, honey."

And I did.

After a few minutes, everything went away. Carol was crying, and I hugged my mom very tight. And then, after the knocks went away, we spent a couple of hours inside the back room. My mom brought papers for drawing, snacks to eat, and we sat together for hours.

I glanced over at dad every so often. He looked so protective with his gun by his chest, but I didn't think of it much. Every so often, he would get up and check outside but never really said anything else. It didn't matter to me, though. I was having fun with my mom and Carol. Whatever or whoever that was, was gone.

And after a couple of days, Mom was talking to the neighbor in the kitchen, and I heard everything.

"The children…," said the crying neighbor.

"How many were there?"

"Twenty-six." she sighed.

The bus that was on its way from Sacramento to pick us up was high jacked when entering Stockton. Twenty-six children went missing that day and were never found.

Twenty-six children from the ages of three to twelve went missing. Rumors began spreading across the city and in our church gathering. And since the church couldn't find them, they closed their doors. We never heard anything anymore, but people talked a lot.

Some say the bus was driven off a cliff by the San Jose coast. Some say the bus was taken to a government facility up north. Some say it was stopped midway and taken to Mexico for trafficking. But it didn't matter how people assumed it went down. What mattered was that twenty-six children went missing, and those parents had to live with the consequences of their decision for the rest of their life.

Ever since then, one rule stood in effect: *Be home before six*. Now, I understand how important it was to follow it.

CHAPTER 3

"Hey!" Jack shouts.

I see him looking through the rearview mirror, and I realize I am the one he's talking to.

"I'm sorry... I didn't hear you," My voice cracks.

"What's your name?"

"Kate," I answer rapidly.

I keep staring at the mirror, waiting for him to say something else, but he doesn't. And as we pass the city of Wesley, Jack reaches under his seat, pulls a black cloth, and tosses it behind him, hitting Eric on the chest. Eric grabs it and hands it to me, "You can't see where we're going. You have to put this on," he says as I stare at the mask in his hands.

I place the mask over my head. My hands: a sweaty mess. I am suffocating. Air ripped out of my lungs, and I want to cry. I want to scream. The wind is rushing through an open window, and all I want to do is jump out into the road; I'd rather be roadkill.

Praying in silence, I beg most not to throw up right now.

The car drives unstable, and I grab the side of the door to hold onto it. Unsure of what is going on, I clean the sweat that is rolling off my hands. It pours from the back of my knees and down to my legs. But I try to calm myself, counting and hoping that as soon as they get what they want, they'll set me free.

We come to a stop, and Eric pulls the cloth off my head. We park in front of a peach-colored, two-story house. I look around and see nothing but dirt land. The dust settles, and I see a highway up ahead.

We are in the middle of the desert, though. I am sure that the road up ahead is not a common one. Certainly not one that can take me straight home.

And as I step out, I notice there are no other houses around us. This is the only one here. It is separated, away from everything. Oh, no.

Jack opens his door and walks inside the house. And as he steps inside, two guys approach him right away. They hand him a cellphone, and Jack's face becomes unexpressive. Like he received some bad news.

He rushes inside and begins shouting, but the door slams shut. Eric stops what he is doing and waits.

Something is wrong.

He grabs me by my arm and starts pulling me inside, but Jack is coming downstairs as we walk through the door. He walks past us and shouts. Eric lets me go and rushes to him, and Jack is now at the hood of the truck.

Eric takes the cellphone away, and Jack isn't so angry anymore. He looks worried. He closes his eyes and shakes his head. Eric leans in and asks him if he is ok, but Jack doesn't answer. Jay runs to them and helps Jack with a couple of things while I stand there, not knowing what to do.

Jack yells and a guy approaches the passenger's side and takes his phone. The guy walks over and holds my arm. "Come here," he says as he pulls me further inside.

"Tell me where we are," I say, but he doesn't say a word.

"Please, I need to know where I am," I say again.

"Be quiet," he says as we head towards the second floor. He opens a door in front of the stairs. We walk into a large room with a window looking towards the highway, the front of the house.

He sets bottled water on the nightstand and hands me a blanket. And as he walks away, I run to him. "Please, let me go. I'm scared!" I cry as he manages to shut the door beforehand.

I turn around to face the room.

The pressure in my chest is horrifying—a heart attack for sure. I take in a deep breath, but no air comes out, and I slam my back onto the wall.

"My God, no!" I scream.

I can't walk. I can't! I forgot how to! This disturbing feeling causes me to keep screaming involuntarily. I drop to my knees. My fingers claw at my chest, attempting to steal a few bars of oxygen from it, but it doesn't budge.

Oh, the things they will do!

I can never sleep!

No!

No eating, not even a drink! I'd rather die!

"Stop!" I scream.

I try to calm myself down, but it is useless.

What if they walk in and shoot me?

What if they torture me?

I've read! I've read many books! Dad said so himself. The world is filled with Jeffrey Dahmers and Ted Bundys. No one is safe. Especially us, girls! Not here! Not in this world!

I hear footsteps and stand up rapidly. I run to the

door to block it, but I listen to them rushing down-stairs. Then, car lights. I run to the window to see many guys leaving at the same time.

I go to the door and turn the doorknob.

Locked.

I pull it, trying to force it open, but it does noth-ing.

I check the other door: a bathroom.

Another: a closet.

No way out.

I am locked in a house full of strangers. Strangers! Not knowing why they want me here—not knowing when or if I'll die.

I've checked the doors several times now, hop-ing some of them would magically turn into another gateway, but no. Calm down! I can't!

But then,

The house remains silent for hours.

Exhausted, but I will not shut my eyes.

Not here, Kate. Not here.

I push a pillow into my face. I press that thing hard up against my mouth—a scream of desperation leaves me. I drop into the bed and stare at the ceiling. I try to focus on the ceiling fan going in circles and focus on the sound of the air, the dead silence around me.

My eyes get heavy. They shut themselves, but I force them open. I sit up and attempt to keep myself awake. Water helps.

I walk into the bathroom and splash some onto my face, hoping that will help a bit, but it doesn't.

My knees and hips are sore. My arms have bruises, and the screams redden my face.

"Stay awake," I whisper.

I keep convincing myself that everything will be fine, just as long as I stay awake.

And for the rest of the night, I just cry.

I can't stop.

I wish I could call my mom and dad, tell them that I am ok for now. Tell them to head down to Modesto and look for nearby houses in the middle of the desert.

Maybe even to tell them: That they are going to lose another daughter tonight.

CHAPTER 4

The doorknob jitters, and I sit up.

Eric comes in with water, a plate of food and drops it off. I notice something on his face. He quietly places the food on the nightstand and stares at the window. He sighs and that tells me he wants to say something more.

I lift my knees towards my stomach and put my hands over them. I'm waiting.

"We'll bring food at twelve and six," he says.

He grabs a blanket from the closet and hands it to me.

"Please, tell me," I say.

He knows exactly what I mean.

Eric runs his hand through his forehead and looks back at the bedroom door. "I don't know," he says, "Trust me, I want you out of here as much as you do."

He puts up a finger towards his mouth to silence me as he sees my mouth open. "Honestly, I'm just trying to protect you," He whispers. He stands at the doorway and looks at me once again.

That looked like a goodbye. Like I wasn't going to live much longer. I just hope that it is quick. Maybe a gunshot to the head, a broken neck, something fast. I don't want torture.

Please, I don't deserve that.

I've done nothing wrong.

"Please," I pray through a whisper. "Let me die quickly,"

But time has passed, and nothing is going on. No upheaval, nada.

It's been a couple of hours!

There is a yellow glow coming off the light on the nightstand that is soothing. I've always been afraid of the dark, but looking out the window, I can see the moon shining across the desert. I am feeling comfortable enough to lie down.

After all, there is nothing else I can do.

I place my hands behind my head and shut my eyes for a moment. But every few seconds, I open them just to make sure no one is inside. And after a lot of thinking, I get annoyed with myself.

Twenty-five years old and afraid of the dark.

What bullshit! Grow up!

Face the fact that this is my life!

When and if I die tonight, I am not going to beg. I am not going to ask for forgiveness. I am not asking to go home. I am just asking for a quick death.

I turn the lights off.

A great deal of bravery.

Carol was never afraid of the dark. That is when she would shine the most. So why can't I? The room becomes pitch black, and I lie back in bed and stare into the ceiling. Keeping my eyes open, I face my fears tonight.

My palms are sweating. A feeling crawls up my spine, and there is a shadow standing before me.

"Stop being afraid," I say while I focus on the moonlight surrounding the room. I focus on every sound. I tightened my knuckles, trying to hold in screams, but I am suddenly thrown back by footsteps outside my door.

I jump up and stare at the light coming from under the door. I throw my legs around the edge of the bed, but I accidentally pull the cord, causing the lamp to fall into the ground.

The light bulb cracks as soon as it hits the floor, and I stand there in the corner of the room, petrified.

I jump into the bed, pull the sheets over me, and drop inside the covers.

So much for bravery. I'm just waiting for morning. And it does.

The dawn is now glowing, and I stand by the window until a truck pulls up. Three guys walk inside. The door slams shut, and I hear them walking upstairs. They walk past my door, and I press my ear against it.

"What do you mean, what did he do? What could he do?"

"Holy shit, man, I can't believe it."

A few minutes after, they are gone again.

No more darkness.

No more fear. At least not now.

There is no way I can stay here.

I am going home. Dead or Alive.

CHAPTER 5

Ican't tell how many days have passed. All I know is that I have seen several sunrises and sunsets. No one has come by. Well, other than an occasional guy coming in to drop off food and water.

I haven't been able to sum up enough courage to ask where Eric is. But a truck leaves every night and comes back every morning, like clockwork.

Sleeping at night has become a challenge. Every night, I give into the fear and keep myself awake. And when the day comes, I sleep with an eye open.

I am too afraid to eat, so I eat a minimal amount. My eyes are swollen, and my head is pounding from the headaches I've been having. I make myself throw up every day. The nauseous feeling creeps up, and I find myself crying by the toilet.

But today, I have no more tears.

A guy walks in.

He goes towards the window and installs a small black box along the bottom panel of the window. He connects the wire to the windowpane, and the box makes a slight beeping noise.

I see a red light flashing. And when he leaves, I study the wires. I move them around and click on a button on the black box. The box beeps twice and I leave it alone as I see two trucks pull away this time.

I unlock the window and slowly push it up, but a loud beep goes off, and I slam it back down. I walk away from it but I hear footsteps outside my door a few minutes later.

"What are you doing?" Eric asks.

"Nothing," I lie.

"Really..." Eric says while connecting the wire back to the window, "You don't want to do that,"

I don't want to wait anymore. I want to go home. I know two trucks leave at seven in the morning, and they come back at twelve. They must have installed this box to keep me in check since they don't have enough people here watching over me.

Which one can I disconnect without making a noise? I've read enough suspense books to know.

A truck arrives, and I duck down. I see Jack stepping out, and he looks mad. I run towards the door and place my ear against it. There is a commotion outside my door, and within seconds, Jack storms inside my room.

"What the hell are you doing? What the hell are you trying to do?" He shouts.

"Jack..." Eric begins talking for me,

"I am not asking you!" He points to me, "You! I'm asking you!"

I lower my head. "Look at me when I'm talking to you!" he says as I look up.

"It was hot, I-" automatically assuming it's about the window. Jack laughs out loud, and I stop talking.

He knows I am lying.

"Mother fucker... " He laughs as he grabs his hair and pulls it towards the back of his head. Jack walks up to me. I stand with my back against the wall as he is too close. Close enough to smell the alcohol on his breath.

"Look..." Jack says. "I am not going to ask you a question and be lied to. Remember that shit from now on," he says as I tear up. Jack covers his face with his hand as he hears me crying. He runs his hand down from his eyes to his mouth in annoyance.

"I'm sorry, "I cry out.

"You are not answering my goddamn question!" he slams his hands on the wall behind me.

"I want to go home!"

"I have my fucking eyes on her now!" he says to Eric.

"Jack," Eric starts talking as Jack stops, "You know the fucking routine: Food and water! That's it! I'm not dealing with this shit. Get out!" He shouts.

Eric looks at me and then lowers his head. He silently walks out as Jack stands with the door half-open. "You need to understand what happens here when you try to fuck with me. So, you want to find out? Fucking try it again!"

And just like that, I am left standing in the middle of the room. Second-guessing my escape now.

CHAPTER 6

Day twenty-four.

Nothing is going on. I am allowed to wallow in my fear. The agony is overbearing. Not knowing for a second where I am or whether I will be alive when I get out.

But I have faith.

Waiting. All by myself.

What am I waiting for? Who am I waiting for? I have faith that someone is heading down here for me, that I am not alone or without help.

I want to believe that my family is out here looking for me. Maybe even hoping that someone saw me get inside that truck.

Staring out the window as if I can see anything, hoping for a car to pull up, hoping for a horde of people to revolt in front of this peach-colored hell hole.

Maybe they can't see me, so I turn on a lamp and place it near the window for anyone to see. Perhaps then, they can question why there is a light in the middle of the desert, and then maybe, they can head this way enough for me to yell.

I know someone will come soon.

I know it.

I need to believe it.

Believing that is all I have now.

CHAPTER 7

Day thirty-seven.

The lamp goes off.

I don't think anyone will know I'm here, not from my neighborhood anyway. Maybe they didn't see me getting inside that truck, or perhaps they think I'm dead now.

Why save a dead person?

All I know is that the lamp is a useless idea. The freeway doesn't seem so far away. Surely, someone will know I am in trouble if I wave a mirror towards it. A flickering light in the middle of the desert is always alarming.

Someone will come.

Someone will see what's going on.

There are heroes out there.

I think.

There are people out there with good hearts. Someone must help. Life doesn't work this way. Life somehow manages to help when it is needed most.

A stranger has to help. I will go home soon. It might not be easy; it might be a struggle. I am ok with that. I'm ok with a small fight to get back home.

CHAPTER 8

Day fifty-two.

Of course. No one came to help.

I have turned on many lamps; I have waved the mirror an infinite number of times. Not one measly soul has tried to help. This is uselessness at its best.

My parents haven't found me. A stranger with a kind heart hasn't stopped by. I have been locked in this room and mentally beaten.

This place feels like it is part of my body now; my veins run through the walls. Its breathes when I do. We are molded into one and all I can do is stare out the window like I am inside a vortex, a tunnel looking into a world that abandoned me. Life is cruel.

But what did I expect?

I made no friends. No one knows who I am. Even if they did, I pushed everyone away, even Carol.

I have no social life, no peers, not even acquaintances. I don't even have that one bad friend who would turn around and help when needed.

I am stuck inside this place, and I have to get used to that. There is no one out there that is going to help me. The only friends I've made are the worms crawling out of the food I've thrown inside the closet.

CHAPTER 9

"Morning," Jack enters the room and walks towards the nightstand beside my bed. He places a plate of food on the table and walks back but he smiles my way.

He doesn't look angry. I even feel him almost normal. "Jack?" His hand almost touches the doorknob, but he stops. "I'm sorry for bothering. I just want to know if you have any medicine. My head hurts."

Jack stays silent for a moment. Then, he opens the door and walks out, closing the door behind him.

Ok. I guess that's that. A few minutes later, he comes back. He hands me a prescription bottle and gives me some water. I look at the prescription bottle and look for the name of what he's giving me.

"If I were going to give your something that kills you, I would force it down your throat," he says.

I lean back and hit the nightstand with my hip, which causes the bottled water to drop. He laughs, picks up the bottle, and hands it to me. "I'm fucking joking… fuck." He says.

With worry, I put the pill in my mouth and take a sip of water. "You haven't taken a shower since you've been here?" He asks, looking at me. "I use the wipes," I say as he lifts his eyebrow.

He walks into the shower and steps outside, confused. "That doesn't work. I didn't know that" he says as he pulls out his cellphone.

He stares at it and then glances up at me with his eyes. His stares at my hair, my face, and down my body. Then, he gives me a crooked smile.

"You do need a shower…" He says, "come,"

We walk outside and through the hallway. There are two double doors on the right side that are closed. He pushes them open, and they open to another short hallway.

We walk down the hall and into a darkened room.

He turns on the lights, and we are in a big grey room with a large bed to the left, a giant TV installed on the wall, a sofa, and a large window looking towards the back of the house.

Large top-to-floor curtains cover a portion of the window, and I see a TV with multiple views from around the house connected to a small box. He stands next to the bed and drops in it. He takes off his boots and leans back into the pillow. He searches around and picks up a device that turns on the TV.

It hits me.

This is his room.

I am inside Jack's room!

I take a step back and place my right hand behind my back, slightly placing it over the doorknob. "I'm taking a shower here?" I ask as I point towards the floor. He points to the bathroom and signals me with his eyebrows.

I look around the room as he sits on the bed, opens a bottle of liquor, pours himself a drink, and sips it. "Again…" He says disinterestedly. "If I were going to do anything to you, I would have done it already." He says as he mixes his drink with his finger.

He leans back and places his hands behind his head.

"God… do I need to force you inside the bathroom? Fuck. Move. Come on," he says as I rush to it and shut the door behind me.

Dear lord, Kate, what have you done?

CHAPTER 10

A shadow! A blurry object in front of the mirror. Oh, Shit!

I swing the shower door open and exhale as I realize there is no one in the bathroom with me.

My goddamn imagination, again.

I pour a generous amount of shampoo on my palm and slather it on my head. For not a moment of blinking, I hurry. The shampoo falls on my face, and I throw myself back into the water to wash it out. Blinded, I run my hands over my eyes.

They burn! Oh, shit, it burns!

And desperation runs the same.

I peek before stepping out. Just to make sure no one is there. I wrap a towel around me, and as I set my foot on the mat, a knock startles me,

"Kate," Jack calls.

I rush to put on my shirt and pants—a world record, I'm sure.

"Kate…" Jack calls again.

I open the door, but not all the way and Jack sticks his hand in and hands me a t-shirt and sweatpants.

"You're not wearing that same shit, are you?"

"I was," I say.

"If you want to smell like sweat, then yeah…" He says as he shakes the clothes for me to grab them.

And after changing, I open the door to Jack pouring himself another drink. He lies back down against his bed and sips it.

"Now, don't you look nice and clean," he says at me but staring at the television. "You want a drink?" He asks. I lightly shake my head.

"Suit yourself. It's delicious."

He points at a sofa next to his bed and signals me to sit down. I hesitate a bit but slowly walk to it. "Holy shit, you're slow," he says as he smiles.

And for a couple of minutes, we remain quiet.

"Do you like this show?" He says.

"We don't have a tv,"

"Wow, you are *those* kinds of people." He laughs. "Anyway, it's hilarious. This one," He adds, "it's pretty fucking funny. You see that guy? Well, he's fucking nuts. He's the main guy." I look at the tv and see some guy randomly walking into a river. He points at the tv, "You see that? They use that shit to call ducks, fucking weird, right? Why do they want ducks? Who the fuck buys ducks?"

He turns to me, and I lower my head. He lifts himself and prompts himself up using his elbow. "Seriously, relax. I'm not going to do anything to you." He says and then continues laughing, "Look! That guy right there. He's going to jump into the fucking thing for a fucking duck. A duck! Who the fuck?"

His phone rings.

He looks down at it and then leans his head back, annoyed. He presses a button, places it on the side of the bed, and continues at his amusement. Seconds after, the phone rings again. This time, he sits up, slams his hand over the phone, and answers.

"What?" He pauses.

I can hear the other voice shouting.

"She's here. ...No, taking a shower. That shower doesn't work," He places his drink on the nightstand, leans up, and sits at the edge of the bed to look at me.

"Why the fuck are you asking so many goddamn questions?"

Jack isn't laughing anymore. I quickly stand up and ask if I can go back to the room, but Jack looks at me, points to the couch, and I sit again. His demeanor changes right away, though. His face is not entertained anymore. He is infuriated. I can tell by the way his hands move and the movement of his lips.

And I want to be away from here

The voices from the duck show aren't enough to cut this feeling inside me. I can hear screams inside my head, and I am worried. Jack doesn't lie down. He doesn't lean back. His drink remains untouched, and I am waiting for the moment he starts yelling at me again. Jack stares at the floor as I hear footsteps outside.

A knock, and he covers his face.

A second knock makes Jack grunt, but he stays there, doing nothing about it. He picks up his drink and gulps it down. The knock becomes a pound on the door, and Jack slams his cup on the nightstand.

"Jack, what are you doing?" Eric says as he peeks inside.

"Watching TV,"

"Kate, come here," Eric calls me, and I stand up but Jack raises his palm, and I stop.

He walks over and places his hand on both sides of the door frame, blocking Eric from coming in.

"Dude, we talked about this," Eric whispers, and Jack laughs.

Eric whispers something else, and Jack leans back, annoyed.

"I haven't touched her!" he shouts.

"Kate," Eric calls me again.

I sit still and don't know what to do. I can't move. I can't even think clearly.

"Here is the thing... "Jack begins talking as Eric pushes his hand out of the way, and as his hand swings down, Eric forces himself inside the room. Jack lifts his elbow and pushes Eric outside and across to the other side, slamming him on the wall across.

"This is my fucking house!"

"Bullshit, Jack! We know you're not all right! This is bullshit! Taking it out on her!" He shouts as he pushes Jack out of the way. The door slams into the wall as he walks inside. "We need to go, come on," Eric says as he grabs my arm but Jack comes in laughing. "We were just watching TV," he says as he picks up his glass and raises his hands. Eric looks at me and looks back at him, "Jack, you're drunk,"

"I haven't done anything to her, have I?"

"I know you're angry, dude," Eric says. Jack's smile becomes a straight line across his mouth.

"Drop it," he says. Eric picks up my dirty clothes and hands them to me while looking back,

"It isn't going to help you if you hurt her instead,"

"I said drop it,"

"We are all fucking sad…." Jack covers his face, running his fingers through his face.

"Son of a bitch! I haven't done anything to her! Tell him!" He turns to me, "Have I touched you?" I shake my head. "See?!"

Eric remains calm and grabs my arm again.

"What are you planning to do?" Jack swings his arm across and slams his hand across the doorframe. He storms out of the room, slamming the door shut, leaving Eric and I alone inside his room.

Eric walks outside, closing the door behind him. I hear mumbling and back and forth arguments. I try to make sense of their conversation, but it is tough to hear with the damn TV going on in the background.

Within a few moments, Jack comes in and slams the door shut as sits on the bed. He isn't ok. I keep looking at the door to see if Eric comes back, but he doesn't. He glances over at me and takes another sip,

"Relax!" He shouts, and I jump but then, I lean back. Silence.

"You're not relaxing…" he mumbles, and I turn my head away. I try to by staring at the tv, but I can't. I keep fidgeting with my clothes, and Jack notices.

"Get your shit," he says as he walks into the hallway and Eric is nowhere in sight. Jack walks through the doors and back to my room. And as he swings the door open, he asks, "Do you need water?"

"No,"

"Food?" I shake my head.

He holds the door, and I walk past him. He reaches over the door and locks it from the inside. He stares straight into my eyes, and I stare back, knowing he has something to say, but he doesn't.

He smiles and then closes the door.

And I am back again inside my room, alone.

Finally.

CHAPTER 11

There are voices outside my window. I walk to it and notice Jack, Eric, and a couple of guys getting inside a truck. I wonder if there is anyone else left inside the house. And if my memory serves me, Jack didn't lock the door from the outside last time.

What am I doing?

Am I staying?

Am I going?

I rush to the door and turn the knob ever so slowly. Like a ticking time bomb ready to explode. It opens! I see no one in the hallway.

Oh, my God! They left me here alone and with a door unlocked! This house is empty!

As I walk downstairs, there are two double doors up ahead. I push them open with hesitation. My breathing becomes a little heavier. A kitchen—a beautiful redwood, stainless steel encrusted kitchen with black marble countertops. And across the room, an exit door.

Freedom.

I peak into the living room and through the hallway again, but there is definitely no one around. My legs, a boneless blubber of skin, feel like I was walking on a floor made of marshmallows, melted foam, clouds!

Focus!

My hand touches the doorknob, and I stare for a moment. My fingers grace it, and my throat tightens with fear. This is great. I can feel hell no longer. I turn it, and the door clicks open.

Go for it!

I push the door open, and it dramatically swings across. As it slams on the house, I feel a grin on my face. As if the sun is opening its arms for an embrace, and I am here, ready for a hug. I take a step down, and suddenly, I realize where I am. Run!

I start running with every ounce of strength inside me. The feeling in my chest explodes into multiple. Emotions rush to my face as I feel the wind forcefully pulling me backward. Go, Kate! Go! I scream at myself. I couldn't run any faster. That highway: it glows! It screams at me!

Run! Go home!

And I do. I run without stopping. Like a gazelle running from a cheetah, I am going home. Doubt creeps up on me, and I feel myself slowing down.

No!

My feet begin shaking. And I pull as much force out of me as I can. My feet hurt. My muscles have been weakened, and I am in pain, but I keep pushing. I jump over a small boulder, and I drop onto the ground.

"Argh! No!"

I push myself up, but my hip hurts. My knees are sore, and I grasp at my chest to continue. "Help!" I scream towards the highway. "Someone, help!" I scream.

I can't see where I am going.

"Help!"

I toss my hands from one side to another, hoping to catch someone's attention.

My ankle gives out, and I drop onto the floor once again. My hands grasp at the dirt, and I push through. I must. The dust lifts, and I scream. Rubbing my eyes, I try to get the dirt out, but it is pointless. My lips, my nose, and my eyes are covered in filth, and I start crying.

A panic sets in, and I lift my shirt to wipe my face. But I am too late. My legs aren't moving. My chest is tight, and I can barely walk.

A truck screeches at a distance and I lift myself to keep running, but the engine revs harder and closer every time. They heard me! They're coming!

"Help! Someone help!" I scream.

Within seconds, the truck is beside me. I run in another direction, but the truck swerves and moves to where I am. I turn around, and Jack screeches in front of me. I slam into the hood, and I turn around once again but as I push through bushes, I feel my skin being pierced by every shrub.

"Stop!" Jack shouts, and he revs the engine in front of me. Like he is going to run me over, he suddenly stops and I run into the hood. I drop to the floor and attempt to catch my breath.

"I'm gonna run you over if you don't stop!"

I drop my head and stare at my scratched arms. I look at my fingernails, covered in dirt. My hair tangled; the t-shirt ripped.

All signs of defeat.

I move my tongue around and spit dirt from my mouth, and I hear Jack behind me.

"Take the car back," he tells someone.

I turn around and see Eric staring at me with a look of terror on his face. But they leave, and I hear footsteps approaching behind me.

"Start walking," he says as the truck is now at a distance. "Get up!" He shouts.

I force myself up, but Jack pushes me with his foot, and I fall to the ground again. Pain shockwaves throughout my body and I shriek. He abruptly pulls me up and pushes me forward.

"Walk!" Goddamn, this is a long walk back. I keep staring at the house- my greatest defeat and I cant stop crying.

Jack slams the kitchen door open and swings me inside by my arm. I grab myself on the kitchen counter because I cannot feel my legs anymore. He grabs me by my neck and pulls me into the living room.

"Stop!" I slap his hand away, and with a sudden push, he slams me into the wall with his elbow.

"Do you think I'm an idiot?!"

"No! Stop!" I cry.

Then, his face changes again. His eyebrows fall to the side. He grabs my arm, pulls me upstairs and towards my room. He slams the door open and pushes me in. He walks to the sofa and sits on it. Then, he holds his head in his hands, he stares at the floor for a while and then moves his lips.

"Kate, I…" he pauses as a guy opens the door and halts as he sees Jack inside the room.

"Oh, I'm sorry, Jack, I didn't know you were here."

"Where the fuck were you?"

"In the pool house,"

"Next time, keep a fucking eye on the cameras, will you?" he says as he takes the plate of food from the guy.

"Yeah. Ok…" He says as he looks at me possibly wondering why I'm sweaty and covered in filth.

Jack closes the door and walks past the bed. He places the food on the nightstand and starts walking towards the door.

"I'm not hungry…." I mumble angrily and he freezes. I lift my head to see his reaction because I know he is going to be irritated but I don't care.

He turns around to look at me and smiles.

Not a happy smile, either.

He paces towards the nightstand and turns to look at me. And as I look, he lifts his hand and drops it on the corner of the food tray. The food flies across and drops on the floor, breaking and dropping everything on it.

"There. You don't have to eat anymore."

He walks to the door as I wipe tears off my face.

"And stop fucking crying. That shit annoys me!"

CHAPTER 12

I wish I knew how to protect myself. I wanted to learn, but my dad said there would never be a reason to. He told us we were never going to be in danger. That if we were in the house, we were going to be safe.

I've never held a gun or even punched someone in the face. Even when Carol and I fought, it was mere discussions. My dad always kept the ultimate power. If we needed discipline, he would be it.

Maybe he was just too afraid to teach us. Perhaps the thought of us fighting was too dreadful to him. My dad only used his shotgun to scare people.

When someone new would approach us, my dad was already at the door with a gun in hand. I don't think he ever actually shot anyone, but hell, he protected us. And we knew it, too.

I understand what he must have felt, though.

Knowing that our society was going to shit was important enough to panic.

My grandpa and my dad always talked about it. They needed to keep us safe at all costs. They said that America failed because we gave everything to the government. Without hesitation, too. We were all too dependent on them. And when the government failed, we were left to pick up whatever it was we could live on.

The US lost control of their people. Companies were far too powerful to stop. The president decided to step down, and no one was ready to replace him. And those who did want to control, made everything worse.

When Elton Graze was elected president in 2038, my dad said, he had promised security and promised big changes. Businesses were going to grow once again, and people saw hope. They loved him. But sadly, Elton Graze was assassinated just weeks before he took office.

It was December 12th, 2038, when Elton Graze was heading to Sacramento. Everyone in America was tuned in to watch President-Elect Elton Graze speak in front of thousands of hopeful Americans. When he stepped up onto the platform and took a microphone, gunshots were fired.

Dad said he shut the TV off and decided to sleep

early that day. Mom, on the other hand, told me he didn't sleep at all. She said he was up walking around the house during the night. She said he walked into my room and sat on my bed for hours. He didn't want to leave us alone anymore.

My dad threw away all technology and cut us off from the internet. We were all ok with it except Aunt Megan. But this didn't matter to my dad.

To him, we were all safe from danger now.

Daddy, I need you right now.

CHAPTER 13

Midnight, they leave. No trucks. 3:20 AM, they come back. One truck.

My notetaking isn't impressive. All I have managed to write down are the times they usually are here. So much for Sherlock on his mystery.

Not a mystery at all, really.

Slam!

Wait. Are they leaving again?

That's odd.

Not their usual routine. I check my notes. Sherlock Holmes has entered the arena, and I am destined to find out more.

I make my way to the door and walk into the hallway. The room to my left is closed. I wouldn't dare try to go through Jack's double doors again, so I am heading downstairs. Right beside the stairs is the basement. I place my ear on the door and hear a machine beeping, so I turn around.

The wind is rushing through the windows, and every little noise startles me. I peek around and look into the living room. I never noticed how beautiful this living room is.

Red sofas surrounded by tall windows. A fluffy white carpet beneath a coffee-colored table. These boys sure have a decorative taste. It is rather sad, though, that there is nothing but empty liquor bottles and cigarettes everywhere.

But what is there to do here on a lonely island?

Oh no.

The dining table has a couple of laptops opened.

Crap!

I slowly make my way into the kitchen and notice the exit door once again. The itch comes upon me. That tingle that tells you that sweat is undoubtedly coming. I stand before the door and admire the out-side. Without thinking, I turn the doorknob.

Much more careful than before.

I stand outside with my chest puffed up. Like my dad holding a shotgun, I have mine. Strong. Des-tined. Much more confident than before. A breath of calm. Don't make a scene.

Slowly and quiet. I make my way to the side of the house where the road is, and I halt by a truck parked on the side.

Goddammit!

Someone is here!

Oh no!

A pause to breathe. Just walk back, slowly. Walk into the room and shut the door.

Call it a night, Sherlock.

I turn the doorknob.

Closed! Holy shit!

What am I supposed to do?

Walk in through the front door as nothing happened? I can't be seen.

I can't!

My heart is going to burst.

I hide behind the truck, peeking through the driver's window towards the house, trying to catch a glimpse of someone nearby. But something else catches my eyes.

Keys.

No… I can't do it! But I can't go back inside. If I get caught, I am going to die.

Shit!

What do I do?

My brain is screaming to go inside. But my heart pleads. It seeks freedom. This car is a blessing. And I see a shining flicker coming off the keys. I open the door and sit. I run my fingers through the keys, so coy.

I turn the truck on and the engine roars. Breathing fire from within, it rumbles inside my chest. I turn around, stare at the kitchen, and then I floor it. My foot pressed down into the metal that I could feel the fuel burning underneath me. I make my way to the road, and I keep pressing the gas, but I scream as I see two posts up ahead.

A flashing red light blinks through the night, but I ignore it as I fly by them.

I did it!

I am going home!

Beep!

"What?!" Desperation. A second beep goes off and then a voice, "Vehicle shut down in five minutes, press control button on your remote device to cancel,"

"What does that mean?!"

My foot still pressed up against the pedal, but the truck seems to lose power. "No! Please! No!" I scream again. I slam my fists onto the steering wheel, but it was no use. This truck is losing as much power as I am losing hope.

"No! Please!" I scream again.

An utter failure. I look up and scream as I run over a big rock. The truck swerves and I slide to a stop. I push the door open and run. The highway! It is so close; I can feel it!

No…No!

"What is this?! What the fuck is it!" I drop in front and see that this isn't a highway.

It was a mirage. The entire area is inside a concrete wall. The concrete wall is covered in cameras and barbed wire.

I planned an illusion! A dream of freedom turned into a nightmare. I was lost even before I knew there was a chance. A heaviness sets in, and my chest feels empty. Realizing that there is no way out even if I tried.

I'm tired. It's true.

I'm tired of fighting.

I see headlights coming my way. But my tears are many that I can't make out who it is. The trucks stop, and I am on my knees, looking away. All I can hear is the footsteps behind me. He pulls me up, whoever he is, and pushes me inside the truck. Another goes and checks the truck I probably destroyed. And just like that, I am on my way back.

No notes this time. No mystery.

Just me and possibly my grave.

CHAPTER 14

I am not sure what is worse.

Does jumping off a plank into the shark-infested water worse than a pirate killing you?

Which is less painful?

Which is quicker?

And can I trade places?

Jack is sitting on the sofa inside my room when I enter. Fuck.

The door shuts, and I turn around to stare at him. His lips pressed in a fine line and his foot jitters. I can feel the scorching energy coming off his body.

"Jack... " I say as he lifts his finger to shush me.

"You don't talk. I do", He says. "I fucking told you," he says in a calm voice but he stands and walks towards me.

"I want to go home!"

"If you attempt to leave one more..."

"Fine!" I shout.

A final desperate attempt to feel in control. "Fucking do it!" I yell, but he remains calm. I open the door, and Jack slams it with enough force to almost break it. And I drop down.

"I'm sorry," I sigh. "Please, don't hurt me," I look up at him, and he steps back.

"Why are you keeping me here?" I shout.

He walks away and crosses his arms. He leans against the wall and smiles like mocking me or amused at my misery.

"Jack…" I sigh. "I want to go home, please…."

Jack sighs and comes towards me. He opens the door and walks out without saying anything else.

Without an answer.

Without anything.

I am left alone without a fucking answer! Why am I here?! Why?!

Why haven't they left my body in a ditch?!

Why haven't they killed me?!

My jaw clenches. I bite my tongue and sock the door enough to make an echo outside. I keep socking it until I fall back.

Despair hurts. Like a thousand bugs crawling on my body, I drop to the floor and begin wheezing.

It aches.

My chest hurts, my shoulders and back is killing me. Every part of my body feels like it wants to break apart.

The room is spinning, and I turn around as every piece of food inside me comes out—the smell of throw-up causes me to continue.

I am going to die. I try to make sense of it all but everything I want to do is wither away, dissolve and vanish. I try to breathe, telling myself to calm down but there is nothing I can do anymore.

I lie here for hours, waiting.

Waiting is worse than dying.

No sharks. No pirates. Desperation does it all.

The sunshine radiates through the mirror, and I notice it sparkles around the room.

But the sunrise is as dark as I have ever seen it.

CHAPTER 15

I think the sun has melted my skin off. It is hot, and I feel like I've been slow cooking since the morning.

What time is it?

Oh, yeah.

I remember now. It doesn't matter here in a…

A prison.

Worse than a prison.

I hate this place.

Detest it. I don't want to be here anymore.

The curtains are draped over the sofa, and the rod is almost at my reach. I pull it off. Like a baseball player during the 1980s, I swing it. The lamp breaks instantly, and the sound of the light bulb shattering causes me pleasure—a great feeling.

I don't know why, but years of pent-up aggression overcomes me. This isn't only because of Jack. It is because of my sister, my mom, and because of my dad. Being shut down when wanting to speak, being under the shadow when I tried to shine, and not saying a word without repercussion.

I am done!

I punch the window aggressively, and it beeps.

Beep!

"Shut up!"

Beep!

"I said, shut up!" I swing the rod at the black box again, and it cracks immediately. I yank the cords out of the window, and I feel a sudden sting on my right arm. Shit!

A piece of shattered window stuck on my arm. Oh shit! I need a bedsheet—something to soak up the blood.

Argh!

Fucking thing! Son of a bitch!

Why does nothing go my way?!

I lift my foot, and I slam it into the closet. One of the doors breaks instantly; the other is hanging by its metal brackets. I stand and tug on it with brute force. Or any energy left in me.

And when it rips off, I swing it and slam it into the wall, cracking the drywall.

I rip the bed sheet and shred it. I slam the pillows into the concrete wall, and feathers fly across the room. I grab the rod and break the rest of the window and mirrors around. The room is my arena, and I am the monster.

Consuming it with anger challenges me.

It represents everything I do not want to be.

The poor room doesn't deserve it.

No.

Jack deserves it!

A haze. Oh, no. The room circles my head, and I drop on the floor again, watching it spin. The only thing comforting me is the isolation- my friend.

A deep breath with every cycle.

Knowing they will come soon; I close my eyes with a saddened smile plastered on my face.

CHAPTER 16

Is it really night time?

Have I been passed out that long?

I turn my head and notice bloodstains on the carpet. My arm is still bleeding. I pull the glass stuck on my arm, and I shriek.

"Oh, my God!"

I rush to the bathroom, press my fingers on it and run my cut underwater. I am desperately looking for something to stop the bleeding.

Oh no. I can't call for help.

The room is atrocious.

Destroyed.

Just calm down. It will stop. Don't call for help. But the bleeding doesn't stop.

"Kate..." Eric stands over me with a towel over my hand. "Are you alright?" He asks.

He helps me sit up, and I feel a night breeze through the broken window.

"Jack asked me to come check on you," he said. "Are you ok? You passed out," I look around, disoriented.

He places a gauze pad over my cut and presses harder with his fingers. I flinch, but he continues. Jay freezes as he walks in. "What the fuck happened here?" He asks as Eric shrugs.

Eric stands up and walks up to Jay. They whisper something I can't understand, and Jay walks out right.

"Take a shower, Kate. We will clean up before Jack comes home,"

The shower doesn't help. I still feel a daze. The bathroom mirror is covered in fog; I slide my hand over it. Regretting it at an instance.

I look terrible.

Dark circles have set beneath my eyes, and they show a lack of willpower. My face is pale. My lips, once red, are now dried and split.

Dreadful.

I feel deformed.

I touch my cheeks, and then I feel my lips. I let the towel go as I stare at my body. I don't have the perfect body. I don't have the perfect face, and I've never been the prettiest. But just maybe…

No.

You are ugly.

I see the shame. I am ugly and disgusting. The skin in this body doesn't belong to me. I feel like peeling it away.

What more for someone who hates her life?

And I hate my life; hate it all. I deserve this. I really do. I hate myself for everything I have put myself through. I deserve to die and more.

Somehow, the pain in my arm is not the same as the pain I feel inside. I wish people could see how ugly I am on the inside. My pretty eyes are covered in envy and judgment. My lovely body is decaying from the inside. Maybe I can. Perhaps I can make myself as ugly for them to see.

I push the soap dispenser and it falls. I pick the sharpest piece of them all. I feel the edge with my fingertip and close my eyes as I start crying.

I want to do it.

The tip of the broken glass is now at my face. And then, I open my eyes. My hand shakes as I press it into my cheek. The sharpest piece breaks off and falls into the sink drain. I cry as I keep pushing it into my face, and I bite my lower lip, holding it from screaming. The glass slips off my hand and falls onto the floor, shattering it completely.

What am I doing?!

Why am I doing this?!

I love myself; I care for myself!

Why am I hurting?

I did nothing wrong.

"Kate," Eric calls as he tries to open the door. I slam the door shut before he sees anything, and I get dressed quickly.

"Open the door, Kate," he says, and I do. I stand back as Eric looks at the floor and the broken pieces of glass.

"What are you doing?" He asks as he stares at my cheek.

"It slipped from my hands," I lie again.

He walks up to me, kicks the glass to the side, and grabs my arm. He pulls me out of the bathroom and closes the bathroom door. He doesn't take my lie.

He knows.

He shakes his head and pulls out his cellphone.

"Eric…" I whisper.

Eric glances at me and shuts the phone.

"You're not ok…." He says.

Jack walks in moments after and stands at the door. He looks around the room, looking at the mess that Jay is cleaning up. He walks around and picks up the broken rod. Then, he walks inside the bathroom and walks out. I can hear the crunches of glass as he walks, and he mumbles something and turns to me.

Jack rapidly walks up to me, but Eric reaches to grab him. Jack swings his arm loose as I pull away but Jack grabs me by my t-shirt and pulls me close to his face.

"You better watch that goddamn attitude of yours. Look at what you did to my house!"

"What about your fucking attitude!" I shout back. He leans back. His eyes open wide, and I know I fucked up.

"What about mine?" He says.

"Jack…" I sigh.

Fix it.

Don't make it worse.

"I'm sorry," I sigh.

A burst of laughter. He turns around as if he is going to walk outside, but then he walks to me, "Is this fucking funny to you?"

"No," He pulls me by my shoulder.

"Stop touching me," I shout but he doesn't stop.

I lift my hand and smack him on his face. He stands back, shocked, and I drop to the floor. I look at his lips, and I know I need to go away. Right now.

I jump up and lock myself inside the bathroom.

"Open it!" Jack's voice echoes inside. I sit on the toilet and cover my ears.

"Open the goddamn door, Kate!" He shouts.

I hear Jack walking away. There was an eerie silence in the bedroom. Not even a few minutes later, I hear Eric shouting, and I stand up. I place my back against the farthest wall away from the door and a loud bang breaks the door open.

I scream and cover my ears.

The loud bang makes my ears hurt and I hear nothing but a high-pitched sound. The dust settles, and I see Jack in the doorway with a gun.

"Jack! No!" I scream.

He pulls me out of the bathroom. Jay and Eric shout at him as I try to pull away. He drags me to the window, and he breaks the rest of the window. He grabs me by my hair and sticks my head out. And with his hip, he pushes my body halfway out.

I shriek. A loud enough scream to get the others out of the house to see.

"Stop, Jack!" I hear them shouting.

I am hanging halfway outside. If it isn't for Jack's grip, I am going to fall.

A sound.

A metal click.

What…

"What the fuck are you doing?!" Eric shouts.

"Jack!" I scream. "Please, I'm sorry! No, please don't shoot!"

"Don't touch me!" Jack shouts to them inside.

A struggle.

They are desperately trying to get me inside the room. Eric pulls Jack's hand away from my head, and I drop in the middle of the windowpane. I quickly pull myself inside and crawl to the corner of the bed.

I lift my knees and cover my head like an ostrich during hunting season. And for a moment, I lose all hearing. I wipe my face as I see Eric and Jack shouting at each other.

Oh, my God. This is it.

Right here.

This is the moment.

"I'm not gonna shoot her! Get the fuck out of here!" Jack shouts.

Jack dusts himself and takes a deep breath. He regains himself, and Eric starts to walk towards me.

"I will shoot her if you touch her," he says, winded. Eric halts, turns to Jack, and looks back at me.

"Jack, I'm…." He starts but Jack shakes his head.

"Get out. I am not going to hurt her." He says.

Jay walks up to Eric and pulls him away, and I stare at them, leaving and closing the door. I look up and then back to Jack, who is standing by the bathroom.

"You think I'm playing games with you?" I stare at the gun dropped on the floor and look back at Jack again, but he notices.

He smiles and kicks the gun towards me. The gun slides across the carpet, and it hits my foot. I clean the tears off my face and stare at it.

"See? You keep trying but let me tell you. You're not gonna make it if you keep fighting,"

He picks up the gun and walks away.

"This shit better be clean in ten minutes,"

CHAPTER 17

Carol always managed to pull me out of danger. She knew how to talk to people and if we ended up getting in trouble, she had sneaky ways of getting out of it.

And she loved trouble.

She didn't always hang out with the best people, but I always tagged along. I am not sure why; maybe I felt I needed to protect her. Perhaps I wanted to feel what she felt. But I was always afraid of her adventures.

She was daylight glistening throughout a shining waterfall and I was inside the cave.

We were the perfect ying-yang.

Somehow, we ended up at parties nearby. I am not sure how she got invites, but she did.

"Let's go," She said one night, "nothing fun here!" We walked to alley close to our house. Our house was a few doors down and we snuck behind a few bushes, like children playing hide and seek.

Being outside that late at night was never a good thing in our neighborhood. It was either people looking to steal cars, buy drugs, or check for open windows but not our house.

My dad knew better.

A tall chain-link fence surrounded our house—all around the four corners wrapped in barbed wire. Carol could climb the fence, where we had removed the barbed wire, and open it for me pretty quickly.

Carol climbed that night when two cars pulled up a few houses down, right where the party was. Carol jumped down right away. She dropped to the ground, and we remained quiet, trying to blend in with the darkness.

Screams.

We stared at each other, and we knew I was in danger. Carol jumped on her knees and tugged on the lock. The keys dropped and she panicked. "Carol..." I said. "Stop! We can't do anything else! Just freeze!" I said. "Oh my God, I'm so sorry!" She cried, looking that way.

Screams again. She looked around for the keys and when she found them, she opened the gate, and we froze as we heard someone in the bush behind us.

"Please..." He said. "No, don't be scared," He

came out of the bushes with his hands up. The cars screeched out, and we were left there, in darkness, with a man—an unknown man with beautiful eyes.

"Who the hell are you, and what are you doing here?" Carol shouted. "I'm hiding," he said.

She pulled me and slammed the gate shut.

"I'm sorry I scared you. Those cars are hell, man,"

"You need to leave," I said.

"Wait, he's just hiding, Kate," She noticed his hand was bleeding and he pointed behind him. "The bushes, man," he said as Carol inspected his injury.

"Carol!" I said,

"Kate, he needs help!"

She pushed me aside as she grabbed his hand and began walking to our house. We sneaked into the kitchen and to Carol's room. She locked the door behind her and pulled out a bottle of alcohol.

"My name's Derek Shiner," He whispered to Carol and her eyes flourished. She wrapped his hand in a gauze pad as she smiled, "I'm Carol and she is Kate".

"Well, Derek..." I whispered. "It's almost two in the morning and my parents are asleep. You need to go," I said.

He stood up and quietly walked to the door.

"Right. Thank you,"

We watched him run into the street, and I stared at Carol, who was staring into the darkened streets,

"Take that smile off your face," I laughed, and I pushed her towards the house.

"Isn't he beautiful! Did you see those eyes?" She said.

"He does have pretty eyes,"

"Pretty? He's gorgeous! Oh, I have to see him again!"

"See him again? Didn't you learn your lesson?"

"What lesson?"

"How dangerous this all is!"

"Oh, come on, Kate, they didn't catch us,"

"But that was too close, Carol,"

"Live a little, little sister. Someday, you'll be caged up with some guy that dad picked out for you, and you'll wish that you'd lived a little right before the ball and chain,"

"A ball and chain isn't all that bad when you're safe,"

"A ball and chain is a ball and chain, whether you want that ball and chain or not"

Come to think of it, that wasn't keeping me safe at all.

CHAPTER 18

"Omg, what are you doing!?" I scream as I see Jack hovering over me. I lift my hands up in front, blocking him.

"You didn't do what I told you to do," he says, looking around.

"I know. Sorry! I'll do it right now." I lift and pick up the bed sheets off the ground. He checks his phone and walks to the bathroom. He stands at the entrance and signals me to go to him. I peak inside the bathroom and Jack points to the mirror. He picks up a glass piece with a bloodstain on it.

"Why didn't you do it?" He asks as he touches my cheek.

"What?"

He reaches over and grabs my arms to pull me in, "Ouch!" I grunt.

"Why the fuck would you flinch at me grabbing you like this, but you are OK doing it yourself?"

"I wasn't going to do it,"

"You weren't?"

"No."

"Then why the drama?"

Jack shakes his head again, picks up a piece of glass, and hands it to me.

"You'll be doing me a big ass favor…" He grins as he walks out, and I stare at the piece of glass in my hand. For a moment, I wanted to answer him, but I didn't have an answer. I didn't know what to say.

I hear glass pieces falling into a trash can and I turn to see Jack adjusting the curtains on the window, he picks up the chair and tosses the broken lamp on the sofa beside my bed.

"I'm your maid now or what?"

"Excuse me?"

"I'm picking this shit up for you?"

"I'm gonna do it."

"I don't see you doing it,"

I walk to the closet, pick up the broken piece and place it on the wall. Jack walks by me and picks up the broken closet door and tosses it near the door.

He shakes his head and laughs.

"Why are you helping me?"

He smiles and gives me the bottled water to put near the bed.

"It's basically my fault that you went nuts. Actually, it is pretty amusing to know you went ape shit on my room," He laughs.

"That isn't funny"

He rolls his eyes as he takes the rod out of my hand, but I hold onto it a little tighter, irritated by his stupid remark.

"You're going to use it on me?"

I stare at it for a moment and let it go.

"No," I mumble.

"You want to"

"No, I don't."

"Come on, just a tad bit,"

I shake my head.

"Come on…." He insists.

"Ok, I do."

"Ballsy"

"What do you want me to say?"

"I'm trying to make this cleaning interesting. I'm tired of everyone being so goddamn serious around me,"

"Well, you aren't all sunshine yourself. Besides, I am…"

"I know, I know… you're being ripped away from home, away from family, friends, and all that jazz…"

"I am, and I don't even…"

"I know, you don't know why."

"I don't"

Jack pauses.

"You really need to take care of that cut," I lift my arm to see and run my fingers through it.

"Looks pretty disgusting," he says as I stare for a moment. He catches my prolonged stare, and he makes a face,

"What?"

"You're bipolar, for sure," I tell him.

He lets out a laugh. A laugh that tells me he found what I said amusing, but I know it's probably because I am right. He throws the pillow onto the bed, picks up the bloody rags off the floor, and hands them to me.

"Baby, you don't even know," He smiles as walks to the door.

"You're hungry?"

"No" I say with stern voice.

"You know, people used to say please and thank you before. I'm not sure why people lost basic manners …" He gives me a crooked smile. Letting me know that he meant me.

"Thank you for keeping me away from my family and my life,"

"You're welcome," he winks and walks out.

CHAPTER 19

They only bring in food once a day now. They know that I'll just toss it into the corner, slumped in the back, growing mold. The cut on my arm is healing but not as well as I thought.

I keep peeling it. This is the only enjoyment I have- to peel the scabs off my wounds.

It's been seven days since I trashed the room. The room is clean, the bathroom is spotless, and Jack hasn't come by to check on it.

The days and nights mix, and I have no idea of the time of day. It doesn't matter anyway. The room is brightened by the moon, a crisp blue color. It's funny how the room changes throughout the day. One moment, it is a bright yellow light embracing every corner and another, a dead blue lighting in the darkness.

Every sunrise signifies a change; it makes me hopeful that I'll get out of here alive one day. But just as the light beats the night, I am confident that I'll beat the darkness of my situation. But every few hours or so, the sunset comes and with that, goes away my dreams.

Darkness always comes back. Some days, it comes more potent than others. And I am left to run under the blankets and cover my head.

At this point, all I have are daydreams—conversation with loved ones, what-ifs, and possible outcomes. Sometimes, I'm convinced that I am crazy. But sometimes, this is what keeps me sane during the day.

But always never-ending.

And then comes guilt.

Like death, it inevitably comes up. I have an overwhelming feeling of guilt. I've spent years telling myself that Carol and my Aunt Megan were crazy. That their moments of daydreams were false and would only cause them to go mad. And here I am, clinging to the last bit of imaginary scenario where I will be happy and safe.

Aunt Megan was my dad's sister. Freedom was everything to her. More so than Carol. When she spoke, the room was filled with optimism. A great speaker: she kept Carol living. And her adoration was Europe.

"Anywhere in Europe is happiness," She would say.

"Once in Europe, we will reach the American ref-ugee camps and be taken care of. Each of us to have our own homes and begin living life as we should. Don't believe what your dad says. We are birds. People are birds, honey. Birds fly across the sky. They leave the nest and get to live life."

Absurd now.

How I wish I could erase these thoughts. Looking for freedom has made me feel even more trapped. I notice tears falling onto my knees, and I bring myself back into my little world. A little voice inside me tells me I'll make it out, but several others tell me it's not possible at all.

What's that?

Noises outside again. I open the door and slowly walk downstairs and see a group of girls walking into the kitchen.

"What are you doing here?" A guy says as he stops me.

"I'm sorry, I was just hungry."

"Go up to your room. I'll bring you something,"

"I'll wait here, please. I won't do anything. I'm just tired of the room,"

That was easy.

"Please don't move from here. I don't want Jack to

get all mad and shit," he says as he walks into another room. I peek through and one girl notices me.

"Party is outside, dear," she says.

The rest look at me up and down. I assume they now realize I didn't come to a party in jeans, a dirty t-shirt, and no make-up.

"So, you came for the party?" A girl asks me as the others chuckle.

"No," I smile, "I don't think I was invited," I said jokingly. The girls look at each other, and then one turns to me. "You… live here?" She asks.

"I don't live here, but I've been here for two months,"

"Jack allows that?" One girl asks.

And there is complete silence now.

"Well, he's the one that wants me here,"

Their mouths drop. Their faces covered in horror. And I know. Finally, someone who can help. My body tenses. Get the words out, Kate! But then, a whisper that shutters me.

"How could Jack allow that? I thought no woman could come through him after *Lisa*,"

What?

They stare at me, and worry overcomes them. I was right. I am not safe. And they know why. The joke is over, and their facial expression told me every-thing I needed to know.

"Honey, if you don't know the Lisa story, then I would suggest you get your things and…."

"Hey! Stop! Where are you going?" The guy comes back, and I pull and swing my arm away.

"Please, I'm just talking…."

"No. Come on, let's go" He grabs me.

I turn around and run to the group as this guy grabs my arm and stops me.

"I don't want to be here. Please tell someone!" I scream.

"Whoa, stop it. What are you doing?" He yells.

The girls pull back and ignore me. They won't help me! I am being pulled into the hallway, and I see their faces. They are not going to help me!

"Help!" I scream as I see one of them walking over, but they stop her. Why do they stop her?!

"Who's Lisa?" I scream as the door shuts. He pulls me upstairs, but I pull away.

"Wait, please!" I beg as I tug on my hand. "Please…" I yell as he shushes me. He pulls me upstairs and slams the door behind him.

"I suggest you drop that argument. Immediately,"

"I need…"

"No!" He interrupts.

"Please, you have no idea what it feels to be here! This Lisa person might be a reason why I haven't been let go!" He stops and pulls me in front of him.

"Listen, this needs to stop. I am asking nicely,"

"At least help me know why I'm here!" I shout as he shushes me. "Kate, just drop it," he says. He quickly turns around and checks the door, placing a hand on it, sighing.

"Drop it. I'm not going to tell you anything," he says.

"Please, you have no idea how it feels to be here without knowing when or if I'll ever leave,"

"We do know how it feels, Kate. We know Jack and his bullshit attitude… so please. Shut the hell up."

And I stop.

They feel the way I do.

They are trapped here, too, just as I am.

I am not alone, after all.

CHAPTER 20

Lisa.

Who's Lisa?

Why were the girls startled?

Why did they tell me to leave?

Why hasn't Jack said anything about her if it was super important? Eric should have said something by now. Eric said he would help me out. He can help me find out who Lisa is. I must talk to Jack. No, I might ask Eric instead.

She could be the answer to everything I've been wanting to know.

CHAPTER 21

"**I** know. I know. You're hungry,"
I whisper to myself like a lunatic. I can't bring myself to ask for food. They'll tell me to eat the food inside the closet. But my stomach rumbles.

The house is quiet tonight. More than usual, so I make my way down to the kitchen again. Not in the mood to cause havoc; I just want food. The kitchen is silent, and I leave the door slightly open and make way to the fridge.

I jump as I notice Eric is standing behind me.

"Oh, my God. You scared me." I whisper.

"What are you doing?"

"I'm hungry."

He pulls a stool for me to sit on and sits with me. He leans back, grabs a bottle of wine, and pours two glasses. He hands me a lunch bag with Eric's name on it and I eat. "I know you're bored, Kate. We all get bored too," He hands me the glass. "How are you bored? You guys are in and out all the time," Eric laughs.

"We should hire you as security,"

"Seriously, you guys are always in and out? Aren't you doing your thieving stuff? That wouldn't be so boring…"

Eric's laugh goes away, and he remains silent for a moment. He sighs, and I can see his face morph into a worried expression. "I am trying to help you, really," he says. "But Jack, you've managed to catch his attention,"

A big gulp of wine to get rid of that sour note.

"Maybe we need to drink like him, huh? Make this all go away somehow." I say.

Eric laughs and leans back, "But come on," He says as he points at the wine bottle, "That shit is weak," He turns around and grabs a bottle of hard liquor left next to the sink and I watch him pour us a drink. "You're nice, Eric. How did you get involved with this?" Eric spaces out for a moment.

"Do you live far from here?" I ask.

"No, we are all from around here. I was born in San Francisco. Other guys come from Sacramento, Yuba City, Wheatland, mostly Northern California," I nod along,

"What about Jack?"

Eric stays quiet for a moment ; like he never really thought about the answer. "Jack comes, well. You know what? I'm not sure, but I think he was born in San Diego. He comes from Bakersfield, though."

"You guys seem close,"

"Jack's my best friend," His smile drops down into a frown. He rubs his face in a troubled gesture and sighs heavily. "But even as my best friend, he never really told me where he comes from," He stares blankly into the bottle.

"That isn't much of a best friend,"

He smiles, "He isn't all bad,"

"I don't know. He seems bad now."

"I try to help people, not hurt them, you know?" I look into his eyes, and the blue hue turns grey. Sadness. His demeanor changes. Eric is miserable, and I am intrigued.

"Have you ever hurt someone?"

"Yeah, and there is not one day I don't regret that," He stands up and leaves the bottle where he found it. "I-I don't want to hurt people. That's not our thing; I didn't sign up for this shit," He roughly scratches his head and I walk to the other side of the island and sit close to where he is now, but he notices me and calms down right away.

"Then why are you here?" I ask.

"Well," he said. "Jack helped me a lot. I feel like I need to do the same for him right now,"

Dear lord, another broken soul inside this house. He knows it too, and he knows I know. I stay silent but stare. He looks around, uncomfortable. So, I smile and start walking to the door.

"Come on," he says. "Join me,"

We walk out of the kitchen and down to the basement. Eric flips a switch, and as the lights come up, there is a large tv connected to about three other small ones. I look at wires connected to black boxes and papers everywhere.

"What is this?" I ask.

Eric pulls a chair and tells me to sit down. This is uncomfortable. I haven't been in front of this much tech stuff since we've been to a friend's house. But I play along, trying to show that I'm around computers all day.

If my dad would see me now.

A screen lights up, and I see security cameras everywhere: the kitchen, the rooms, the backyard. Another one has the barricades and a pool house.

"I don't believe this. You can see the entire house on these things?"

He smiles and pulls a liquor bottle from underneath the table. "You think we are blind to what goes on around here?" He laughs.

"Oh, my God. Makes me feel dumb for trying to leave…"

"That's ok, I don't blame you," he says.

"What's that?"

A small black box with a red square sits on top of a lock box.

"A mouse?" he grabs an oval-shaped object.

"No, that thing."

"I take it you guys weren't fond of technology?" He asks.

"Not much. Well, we had none. Just basic electricity: nothing connected to TVs or the internet," I say as he chuckles. He plugs in the black box and the screens turn black. He pulls out a green box from the lock box and a small device with wires attached. He plugs that in with all the others and he begins typing.

Typing and drinking.

Drinking and typing.

It seems he forgot I am here because he doesn't speak to me nor looks my way for a while now. His phone rings. He answers, and his voice is even deeper, sterner. A voice that means business, but I ignore it.

He keeps pouring alcohol into my glass, and I keep drinking. By now, I feel pretty warm inside.

Too warm.

Damn, I think I'm getting drunk.

"Hey, do you have it? Outside Marysville, about 20 miles down south."

He connects the computer to another screen. The screen turns black, and he types some numbers in it. Suddenly, the screen beeps, and tons of personal information comes on from several different people.

All by the same name.

Oh my God.

This…

This is what my grandpa used to talk about. Our information. Our personal information is here. Everything for others to see, to have, to use. Exactly why we never used the internet.

They are the reason why my grandpa lost everything.

This is why people lost their homes.

I don't know the face I had when Eric turns to me and quickly unplugs everything.

"OK, let's go back upstairs. I think you saw enough,"

"Come on, please…"

"Come on, please, what?"

"Continue,"

"No, you've seen enough. I made a mistake."

"Please go on,"

"Kate…" Eric says, concerned.

I set my glass on the table and start walking upstairs.

"Kate," Eric calls and I turn around. "Don't tell Jack you were down here,"

"Why are you guys so afraid of him?" Eric laughs.

"Jack? No, we don't fear him,"

"I see what you guys do. Somehow, it is very important not to piss him off." Eric smiles and stays quiet.

"No, that's not it,"

"Jack makes you guys nervous," I say.

He finishes his glass and wipes his mouth.

"And now, I'm drunk," He stands as I walk back and push him into his seat. He looks at me but doesn't say anything. He leans his head back and shakes it. He looks straight into the ceiling and smiles.

"Eric," I say as he looks at me.

"He is like that because of Lisa, huh?"

"What are you talking about?" his smile disappears.

"Lisa,"

"Stop,"

"What did she do?"

"How do you know about her?"

"Just tell me first,"

He shakes his head and gets up, trying to put things away. I stare for a moment, but I don't leave.

"I don't care, Eric. I want to know,"

He shushes me and we both look upstairs.

"No, tell me why?"

"Someone can hear you, be quiet."

"Why should I be quiet? I'm so tired of being quiet!"

"Because he asked you to," Jack says as he stands by the door.

CHAPTER 22

My body freezes, and my eyes open wide. No courage to look back. All I do is stare at Eric's eyes, locked behind me towards Jack.

"Sorry, man. She said she was hungry, so I offered company,"

Jack walks downstairs and stands behind me. Still, not a single ounce of courage to face him. Eric walks behind me, mumbling but Jack pushes Eric out of the way and grabs me. Like a third grader after recess, I walk shamefully to the room. Thinking he would leave me alone, I stand by the door, but he walks past me and sits on the bed.

"What the hell am I going to do with you?" He says.

"I didn't mean to ask so many questions. I was just...."

A laughter and I stop talking. He looks at the broken window and looks back at me.

"Again, with that fucking attitude!"

"What attitude! I have no attitude! I'm answering your question!"

"Seriously, cut that shit out,"

"Well, I'm just fucking tired of being here, Jack! I have done nothing to you, and you treat me like I stole some shit from you guys!" He lowers his head and pulls his hair back. He walks to me and stops inches from my face, a little too close.

"I'm not going to hurt you," he says "But…" and I push him away from me. He grabs me by my wrists in a joking manner.

"Let me go!"

"No," he laughs.

"Stop it! I'm not Lisa! You need to take your bullshit out on her!"

Jack's laugh stops right away.

Oh, I made a huge mistake. His face becomes blank. His eyes went from humor to dread in mere seconds. I know I stunned him. I was told by the guy and by Eric to shut up about it and looking at Jack's face, I know they were right.

A cold feeling runs down my stomach as I keep

staring at his eyes. Those dead, shocking eyes looking behind me, staring blankly at the wall. Like his soul left his body. I move aside and rush to the corner of the room when he grabs the back of my neck.

With a forced pull, he pushes me into the bed as I scream. He tries to get a hold of my hands, but I don't let him. I shriek and cry for help, but he pulls me up and slams me into the wall.

"Stop!"

I can't make him stop.

"Help!" I shout for someone to hear me, but he is too strong, and I can't scream loud enough.

"Let me go!" I yell as I scratch at his hands.

I drop my body to try and free myself, but it is no use. He grabs my face and I sink my teeth into his hand, and he yells. I throw myself down and run to the door but without realizing it, the blanket wraps around my legs, and I stumble, hitting my forehead on the corner of the bed frame.

I immediately notice blood on the carpet and pain sets around my neck and forehead. I want to move, but the pain stupefies me, and I am gasping for air. My body tightens and I exhale a scream. An agonizing pain settles, and it feels like someone is crushing my head. I can't move.

Jack rushes over and pulls me, but I smack his

hands away. "Fucking, stop!" He shouts as he lifts me and throws me in the bed. He grabs my chin, turns my face to him and runs his fingers through my head.

"Son of a bitch!" He says as I turn my body away. I hold my head, everything is darker, and I can't think clearly. He tries to move me, but the pain is now stockpiled on my forehead.

He walks inside the bathroom, and I try to move, but I am incapable of such. Jack comes over and places a towel on my forehead, and I close my eyes. The pain is numbing me, and I drift to sleep.

Such a beautiful feeling.

"Nope," He lightly smacks my cheek.

"Stay awake." He says as he rushes to the door and shouts.

I am scared of dying. Afraid of being with him. Scared of living, of everything.

What to do?

"Help Me…" I sigh.

He picks me up and instead of going downstairs, he walks towards his room. He kicks his door open and places me in his bed. He gets up and walks around. His face is again serious. His mouth is shut, lips pressed in a fine line. Then, he balls his fists and walks around furiously.

And I start crying.

Jack swings a cup into the mirror with such force that it shatters in contact. The mirror falls backwards, and he slams his hand across a lamp.

"Fuck!" he shouts as the lamp smashes across onto the wall. He grabs a frame and swings it across the room. I am terrified. I don't know what to think. Stuck between trying to survive this and survive him.

What options are there left?

But then he takes a deep breath and comes over. He sits down and keeps breathing. He looks to me and then covers his face with his hands.

"She's not Lisa…" He whispers.

He keeps whispering things that I can't understand and all I want to be away.

"Jack…" I cry.

"Shh…"

He walks into the bathroom and, moments later, comes out with a gauze pad and a bottle of rubbing alcohol.

"Jack…" I lift my hand to push him.

"I wouldn't do that, don't touch me," he says as he pours alcohol into it. He wipes my entire face, my forehead, and then rubs my nose.

"What the hell did you do?" Eric storms inside the room.

"I didn't do anything. She tripped."

"Jack,"

"Don't believe me? Check the fucking cameras."

"What the hell am I supposed to believe here?"

"I told you. I know it's my fault but I'm helping now,"

Eric lifts and angrily slams the door shut. Leaving me alone with Jack again. Why? Why didn't he stay? Jack sighs and turns back to me, rubbing alcohol over my mouth and nose. I lift my arm to push Jack's arm out of the way, but I noticed this is not an alcohol smell, but rather something else. I pull my face back, and he leans in. He smiles and covers my face again with the cloth.

My body feels numb.

"Stop, please!" I yell out.

"Kate," He whispers, "Let go. I'm not going to hurt you," he says as he grabs my weakened arm and places it beside my body.

I start crying because I can't do anything about it. I try to lift my arm, and I fail again. I lose feeling all around my body.

"Please, listen. I'm just trying to help,"

My body feels like I'm drifting into the sea, waiting for someone to come and rescue me, but no one does. I let my body drop to the bottom of the ocean, and I can't do anything, not even reach for the lifesaver right in front of me. I feel as if I'm drowning. As if the ocean is smashing my body between boulders, and I am giving up. Not trying- not even for a single moment of breathing.

CHAPTER 23

Safety is a funny thing.

What is it, anyway? And who provides it?

To us, my dad was our safety. But did it work? Did the years of isolation help? Did the four fences around our property help keep the monsters out?

Jack keeps saying that he won't hurt me, but I don't think he believes it either. Safety is an illusion. Always has been.

When Derek came into the picture, Carol became a one-man girl. She started dating him about two weeks after we met. And while I pictured a boyfriend to be protective, Derek wasn't a safe kind of guy. He would take Carol everywhere, not always the best places, but I think Carol liked that anyway.

Every time he would pick us up, and I mean "us" because everywhere Carol would go, I would go, he looked nervous.

"What's going on?" I asked one night. He smiled at me and turned to Carol. He kissed her while looking around.

Creep.

"Why are you looking around? What is going on?" I said.

Derek looked at me through the rearview mirror and then turned to Carol, "Calm you sister down, please…" he said. I sat back and remained quiet as Carol laughed. There was something I didn't like about him. All the mystery surrounding him was unnatural.

He always kept secrets, always told Carol to keep secrets for him. The least he could do was to let us know where we were going. Every night, it would be somewhere different. Every night, different people.

We arrived at his house and Derek pulled Carol into the back room, and the door closed. I kept staring at everybody drinking, smoking, and who knows what. I didn't mind a drink, but not there.

Not with them.

Not even thirty minutes passed by when a car pulled in front of the house. People scattered, and the door slammed open. We dropped to the floor, and two guys ran to the back.

"Carol!" I screamed. Derek ran past the living

room and outside. The two guys followed, and Carol came out screaming. I grabbed her and pulled her the opposite way.

"Carol! Forget about Derek! Let's go!" Carol rushed over to Derek's car and pulled the keys from under the tire. She jumped on the passenger's side, and I ran to the driver's side.

"Derek! We have to go get Derek!"

"He's gone, Carol! I'm not going looking for him!"

"Turn around, Kate!"

"They wanted him! Not us! I'm not going there!"

I drove towards our house, and Carol kept looking behind her. Pulling around the corner, we see a car at a distance. The lights flickered and sped towards us.

"Carol, they're getting close!" I shouted as she looked behind.

"Maybe it's Derek!" She shouted back. The car pulled beside us, and we noticed it was the guys who stormed into Derek's house. Carol screamed, and I tried to outrun them.

No Luck.

They slammed their brakes, and so did I. Leaving us stuck in the middle of the street. Their door opened, and we saw them step out.

"Kate…" Carol said as she lowered her head. "You have to run when I tell you to. I'll deal with them,"

"What are you talking about?"

"Ok, listen…" She said nervously.

"What are you… wait, what?"

"Derek stole something from them, and they are looking for him."

"What the hell are you talking about!"

"He's…"

"What the hell, Carol!"

"Kate, lecture me when we get home."

"We might not make it home!"

A guy walked up to us and opened my door,

"Why are you driving this car?" He asked.

"We were scared, and we took any car we found," Carol responded. The second guy walked past us and knocked on the trunk,

"Open it," he said as I pulled the trunk lever.

"Why are you guys out so late?" I stepped out, and Carol walked around and grabbed me. The trunk closed, and the guy walked to us, holding a small black bag.

"This can get you in deep trouble," he said as he showed it to us. I looked up at the guy as he handed the black bag to the other one.

"Please let us go…." Carol said, "We are just trying to get home."

"Do you know what this is?" He waved the bag in our face. Carol looked at me, paused, and then turned to him.

"A tracking device, it's called TQ400," Carol answered.

To my surprise, I turned to look at her while she stared at me in silence.

"You shouldn't be involved with things like this," He said as he walked by us towards the front of the car. The second guy passed us and smacked the other's back. He stopped talking, and both left right after.

Carol and I stood there, in silence, as the car took off around the corner. I dropped into the driver's seat and remained silent. I could see Carol's disappointed face. She walked and got inside the car and when she sat, she remained silent for a few minutes. But a rage crept inside my chest, and I couldn't handle it anymore.

"Really?!"

"Look, you wouldn't understand!"

"Why on earth would I?"

"He is just trying to help me!"

"How? He steals! He is stealing from these kinds of people! How is that helping you?"

"Well, he is! You wouldn't understand!"

"Why wouldn't I?"

"Because! Because you like being caged up, Kate! You're a fucking robot! You like withering away, living at home, and living a robot life! You like that! Me? You don't understand me. I like being free! I want to look for a way out, so quit it! I want out of this, and Derek is helping! Go live your caged-up life inside mom and dads!"

I sat back, and for a moment, I went still.

I bit my lips to keep from saying anything else. Carol was right.

I hated going out.

I hated the parties.

I wanted safety; I wanted conformity.

Most of all, I wanted a safe place.

"You're right! I do! I'm never going to your fucking parties again, Carol!"

And at that moment, we separated emotionally.

My older sister was not a sister anymore; she felt different to me.

CHAPTER 24

The water pours.

Soothing, like sweet caress over my skin.

I need this. Everlasting serenity embraces me, and it heals everything it touches.

"Don't move," Jack says.

"Don't!" I shout as I push his hand away.

My head drops underwater immediately, and I notice he was the one keeping my head above water.

The strength in me was used to make Jack go away but not enough to lift myself. I tighten my stomach and pull but I couldn't. He swiftly lifts my head and shakes his head.

"You are severely medicated. Don't do that," he says as he grabs my arm, sits me up, and holds me in place. I stare at him, and he smiles.

"Relax," he says, but I can't keep my eyes away. He

places my back against the wall and reaches for a bottle of alcohol. He soaks the cloth and places it on my forehead again. He runs his finger through it and smiles.

"That's a fucked-up cut," he says.

He moves my hand and asks if I can feel it.

"Yeah," I sigh. He moves my arm up and moves my fingers one by one. He takes out a pill and places it in my mouth. He tells me I should start feeling soon. And after a few minutes, I do.

Finally.

He drops a towel over my shoulders and lifts me.

"Don't let me go," I say but he doesn't respond. He carries me into the room, and I wished for him to take me to my room but no; he drops me into his bed. He grabs a t-shirt and shorts and hands them to me. He moves my hair out of my face and opens my eyelids.

"Can you move your hands?"

I move it slightly.

"You should be good in a few minutes," he says as he places the clothes on the nightstand. "Leave your wet clothes on this bag. I'm gonna take a shower. When you gain enough strength, change. I'll knock to see if you're done," he closes the door, and I hear the shower run.

I stare at my hands, and I try to move them.

Nope. Move! I wiggle my toes, but I feel fragile. I grab myself on his bed frame and pull myself up. My entire energy is set on changing before he comes out. I don't want him helping me at all. The humiliation is frightening me more. I forcefully tug on my shirt, and I manage to take it off. My eyes locked on the bathroom door to see if anything changes.

Ugh! After several attempts, I am finished.

Horribly but I am.

"Are you changed?"

"Yea,"

He walks over and laughs.

"Horrible job," he says as he adjusts the clothes on my shoulder and props a pillow beside me.

"Go to sleep. You'll need a good couple hours to recover for that one," He says as he runs his thumb on my forehead. I lay back as I see him pour himself a drink.

"Want one? Oh, wait. No. Not with that much medication," he says as he sits on the sofa and turns on the TV. Why am I still here?

I want to go away but I know he won't let me. Not with the way I am right now. I turn to look at him, but he is sleeping, now. Then, a deep snore.

Oh good. I can finally relax a little bit. But it doesn't help me. Because I know that when pain goes away, fear always come back. And right now, fear is sleeping right next to me.

CHAPTER 25

Gunshots.

My body shakes, but I can't move. The birds flap their wings fast enough to avoid a bullet, but I find myself stuck in the mud. I pull my leg, and it cracks. My body hits the floor as another gunshot goes off—laughter. I fearfully look around but find no one, the laughter echoes, and I know I am next.

Oh, crap.

I'm still inside Jack's room. I open my eyes and see him laughing. He is sitting on the sofa. And when he walks into the bathroom, I wiggle my toes. I move my legs, extend my arms. I move my tongue and open my mouth wide.

Good, I can move now.

A bottled water is sitting on the nightstand, and I extend my arm to grab it. My muscles hurt. Every part of me is sore, like I've been in a fist fight with a muscled guy.

I hear the door creak, and I pretend to sleep. And a few minutes later, I hear Jack snore once again. I look over and watch him as his hands are crossed across his chest, his face serene and calm- peaceful.

I walk to the bathroom, but I am stopped when I see a notebook by the TV.

What the hell does he write about?

I pick it up and flip it over to look at the back, but a piece of paper falls. I rapidly pick it up and look at it. I instantly freeze, and my heart crushes. I take a step back.

Oh no.

No.

I bump the cabinet with my hip and turn to look at him. Then, I stare back at the paper in my hand:

Derek Shiner (530) 735...

Oh my god, no!

My guts sink to the bottom of my stomach, and I feel nauseous. I hold myself on the drawer, just to not pass out but I can't.

I can't believe it.

No, this isn't real.

This is another nightmare. It has to be! Wake up, Kate!

"What did you find?"

Shit!

When did he stop snoring?! I turn and reach back to push the notebook away from me, but he smiles. He walks over. Not knowing what to do, I remain there—my hand behind my back, slightly pushing the notebook further away. I wish it could suddenly disappear and disintegrate into thin air, but Jack stands in front of me, leans in, and pulls the notebook from behind me.

He walks back and sits on his sofa. He opens the notebook, glances at the piece of paper, and closes it, lightly placing it on the nightstand.

He turns, grabs his drink, and lies back once again. I swear I've been standing here for hours, but it was only minutes, minutes that feel like an eternity. He looks up at me and then back at the TV.

"Go on," he says, but I don't know what to do. I look over at the TV and then look at Jack again, who is waiting. He grabs a cigarette and turns it on.

"You're pissing me off just standing there," he says. "You're not going to ask about the piece of paper?"

I shake my head and then shift my eyes to the TV. He grabs the notebook, pulls out the paper, and waves it,

"Tell me about him," he says.

"Jack, I want to go to my room," He closes his eyes and shakes his head.

"Tell me,"

"Can I please…."

"I don't like waiting, Kate." He interrupts.

Jack places the glass on the nightstand and rests his arms on his knees.

"He used to be my sister's boyfriend,"

Jack looks at the TV, but his face isn't so calm anymore. Basic information is not what he wants. He wants to know everything I know.

"But he's gone. I think." I add and Jack sighs loudly.

"Where is your sister?"

"I think she's gone too,"

Jack walks past me and calls me over. We walk to my room and when I go in, Jack closes the door behind him.

Oh, come on!

"Where is he?"

"I don't know,"

He laughs and covers his face with his palm.

"Really. I don't know where he is or my sister. They both left months ago,"

"Where did they go?"

"I don't know. I didn't talk to her before they left. I don't know where they went or even how they left. She was supposed to call me but never did."

"I don't like being lied to, Kate,"

"I'm not. Look, I wasn't talking to her at the time,"

"What do you know about him?"

"I don't know much. They kept things from me."

"And you're sure you don't know where they went?"

"I don't know,"

Jack bites his lip and rubs his face.

"Do you not like him?" I ask.

He shakes his head, then rests his face on his palm and looks sideways. "I swear if I find him…."

"Well, if you find him, I will ask you about my sister,"

A pause. "What do you mean?"

"I want to know if she's ok,"

"She left with him on purpose?"

"Yes"

"To be with him?"

"Yes"

"You sure?"

"Yes, why do you ask?"

"Let's just say you're having a great time compared to her,"

CHAPTER 26

I can't imagine Carol being in a place like this. I try to shake off the feeling whenever I picture her trapped and imprisoned. If being home was hell to her, what would a place like this feel like? She couldn't last as much as I did.

She always admired and strived for freedom. Aunt Megan and Carol would always fantasize about it. They even played music as an inspiration. I hear her favorite song inside my head—a song about being free and about places to see.

Aunt Megan loved Lynyrd Skynyrd, and that rubbed off on Carol. Well, until my dad thought "freedom music" was terrible for us.

Aunt Megan and Carol would spend hours talking about flying to different countries, living with foreign people, eating exotic foods, and marrying dark Italian men.

"Carol! Come here, hurry!" Aunt Megan said one day.

"Look! A hummingbird!" Carol ran across the living room and jumped onto the couch. Carol loved bird watching, and Aunt Megan loved to see Carol happy.

"You see its wings?" She pointed. "Hummingbirds fly anywhere they wish. They flawlessly travel through the horizon without a single care in the world," Carol's smile was big.

"That's the thing with birds, sweetie. During the darkest winters, they fly away. Anywhere and everywhere they feel safe. And when things get warm again, they simply come back home,"

"Oh, Shut up, Megan!" Dad shouted from the kitchen.

"Pfft," Aunt Megan would scoff. "Your daddy doesn't like birds. He likes to keep them inside their cage or cook them up for dinner," she said to Carol.

"Yeah, daddy!" Carol shouted back.

"Megan, just stop. Don't get these ideas in her head."

"Why not? She's a child, and children should run free and play outside. They should have a haven in the wild," she said as my dad shook his head.

"Well, her haven is here. Stockton. Inside her home."

"Oh, Please…" She mocked him.

My dad walked and grabbed Carol's hand.

"The thing is, Meg. They are not your daughters. They're mine. I decide what their life is going to be," he said as he tried to pull Carol from Megan's lap, but Carol slapped his hand away.

"I want to be a bird, daddy!" Carol shouted. Dad looked at me and frowned. "See what you've done, Megan. Thank you very much."

And I knew what my dad was saying. He didn't want us to leave. He wanted us to be safe. I tried for days to understand Aunt Megan's story.

It was a ludicrous idea for me to leave home in such a dangerous world. I never considered myself to be that free bird that Aunt Megan used to talk about.

I never wanted to travel.

I was content at home, inside a safe place, and with my family.

CHAPTER 27

Jack comes in and tells me to follow him. I freeze and hesitate a bit. It's been a couple days since my accident, and I was perfectly ok with being alone inside my room. The last thing I want is to have another problem.

"I'm not going with you," I say.

A brave act.

"I'm not asking you,"

"But I want to sleep."

"You've slept like twelve hours!"

"Well, if you didn't hurt me, I wouldn't have done that!"

He swings the door open and stands there. "Get over here!"

I walk to him, and we walk downstairs. But then, he steps outside, and I stand by the entry door.

"Son of a bitch, Kate!"

"What?"

"Do you know how easy it would be if you just fucking listen?"

"I don't trust you,"

"I don't expect you to. I'm not Aladdin,"

"Who?"

"What the f… shit! Get inside the truck!"

I pull the door open and jump into the seat. I cross my arms, fold them and he slams the door closed.

"I should be the one scared of being in a car with you with that fucking attitude," he says as he drives away.

I smile and he does too. He doesn't look angry. He looks calm. A face that tells me that I am ok for now. So maybe, this isn't a murder mission. This is just a day out. Maybe. He turns on the radio and I lay my head on the side.

The music; it's amazing. Such a beautiful thing.

Why didn't my dad let us listen to this?

Jack smiles as I turn the button, the one that he used to put the volume up. But then, I notice we are heading towards Sacramento.

And I wonder.

What is he doing?

I see a sign ahead that says, French Camp Road. I sit up straight, and Jack notices. A knot forms inside my throat, and I want to scream.

Is it excitement or panic?

I don't know but I stick my head out the window.

Ah, I can smell mom's cooking from here.

"What is going on?" He asks.

"Nothing," I say. "My house is that way. That's all." He stares back at the road, and I cave into the seat again as he doesn't do anything else.

But this doesn't mean I can't wonder:

I picture it all: We drive off French Camp Road and towards my house. I pass the convenience store, and Jack drops me off. My car is still there, and I feel great. My parents are waiting for me with a home cooked dinner and a set of cleans clothes. I hug them. I hug my mom tighter. My dad looks around for danger, but we are safe. Safe at home, and Jack never returns.

But no.

He keeps driving further away. I turn my face away, arrested by sorrow. I ball my fists enough to turn them white and I breathe. That was just an illusion once again.

Jack gets off the freeway and drives through a

massive yellow bridge. We move through the rubbles of broken trees, and I see a river up ahead.

"Where are we?" I ask.

"You said you felt trapped," he says as he steps out. He empties his pockets, and I stare, hoping not to see a gun. He knows exactly what is going on inside my head because he smiles and shakes his head. "Seriously." He says as he walks around and opens my door.

Jack goes to a bench beside the river, and I notice he left his cellphone and keys on the seat beside me, so I assume he isn't planning to leave me here.

"Fucking shit, Kate," I hear him laugh as he takes out a cigarette and smokes it. I step out and walk up and as I approach the water; I remove my shoes without thinking.

"Be careful. It's strong,"

"Have people drowned here?"

"Yup"

"Is this why you brought me here?"

"Yeah, that's my plan," He rolls his eyes.

His phone rings and he picks it up. I can't hear a thing, but I enjoy the moment anyway. He takes out a little black box and pushes some buttons on it. I'm surprised it doesn't look like a cellphone.

"Why do you need that?"

"Safety,"

"Jack…" He runs his fingers through his face and down to his beard. "Here we go…" He pauses and exhales. "What?"

"You don't seem so creepy anymore,"

"Oh my God…" He laughs.

"What?" I ask as he walks to me.

"Nothing,"

"Eric said you guys have never kept people like me,"

"What do you mean?"

"Kidnapped…"

"You're not kidnapped,"

"I don't have any information for you,"

"I know…"

"I really don't know where Carol is."

"Who?"

"My sister… and Derek"

"Oh, I know that too,"

"They're probably gone. They're probably in Europe, living happily ever after,"

He chuckles.

"She loved her boyfriend," I add.

"Derek wasn't her boyfriend."

"Yes, he was."

"No, he wasn't."

"Why are you so sure?"

"He used her,"

"What?"

Jack shakes his head and picks up the black box.

"This is used to track and transfer information. TQ400, newer model give or take,"

"And?"

"Derek used it to track girls. Girls who would do anything for him. I'm sure your sister saw this plenty of times. If she has one now, you wouldn't need to cry over her. You'd know where she is right away," I lift myself from the floor and stomp to the car.

"Why are you angry?" he laughs and I stop.

"My sister was crazy in love with that guy! Let me have a little bit of hope!"

"You know there isn't hope with Derek, right?"

I attempt to walk away, but Jack pulls my arm and brings me back. "Listen," he starts as I swing it away. "Jack, let me have some hope. Let me live in the illusion that she is ok. That makes me feel better. My sister means everything to me, and I am stuck with you because I went out looking for her."

"I take that as an insult," he says as he crosses his arms. I walk to the truck and jump inside. He shakes his head, walks to the driver's side, and places the box under the seat.

"Whatever you say, Kemosabe. She's happy! She's safe! She's all right!"

"Stop being an asshole," I mumble.

"I know Derek. I know she's not ok."

CHAPTER 28

Carol used to be so happy. And she was happier with Derek. Well, until the night we got caught.

Carol and I drove in silence after we got stopped by the two men. I kept staring at her fingers. They moved in circles, one around another. She often looked back, looking for any sign of Derek but every light post we drove by lit the tears running down her cheeks.

I parked on the corner and walked to Carol's side to pull her out. I dumped the keys inside the car and started walking. The sun was beginning to shine upon us, and I knew my dad would wake up soon.

We jumped the fence, and as soon as my feet hit the ground, my dad cleared his throat. We turned around to see my dad standing by the doorway with the shotgun in his hands. The look of disappointment.

Another letdown.

He stormed inside the house as my mom came

to ask us where we were. And as we walked into the kitchen, Carol spoke,

"Dad,"

Smack!

A slap across her face.

"Now you put Kate in danger?!"

"Dad, you know I can't stand being inside the house all the time!" Carol cried.

"Who gives a damn? Think of your sister! How stupid of you to put her in harm's way!" He shouted back.

"They didn't even do anything to us!" Carol yelled.

"Them who?" He asked. "What happened?"

Carol stayed quiet, and dad looked at me.

"I am getting tired, Carol," he said, disheartened.

"Dad…"

"It's gone too far. I'm tired of this bullshit,"

Mom sat beside me. I could tell the disappointment on her face, but she stayed quiet. Usually, mom would defend us, but this wasn't ok. Not even for her.

"You are stupid to believe that it is safe out there! Listen to us, please!" Dad yelled.

"Well, that's why I'm leaving!" She screamed.

Dad slammed his hands on the table, shaking the cups and utensils left at the table that night.

"You are crazy! You can't go!" He shouted.

"Why can't I go? Aunt Megan did! She made it! She taught me how to do that; how to get away from all this!" She shouted.

Dad covered his face and ran his fingers through his eyes. "Aunt Megan didn't go to Europe!" Dad shouted.

My mom rushed to my dad and told him to calm down. She patted his chest as he moved mom's hand out of the way. "No, Cristina! They need to know what happened!" He shouted.

"Stop it, Andrew. Tonight is not the time!" she pleaded.

"Today is a perfect time!"

"Andrew!" My mom tried covering his mouth, but he pulled it away as Carol stood up and started walking to her room.

"Well, it doesn't matter because I'm leaving!"

"No, you're not!"

"Aunt Megan said I would be able to stay with her!"

"You won't leave! You're staying here!"

"Why can't I go with Aunt Megan?"

"Because!"

"Because what?"

"Because Megan is dead!"

I can never fully describe Carol's face when dad shouted those words. My mom sat on the table as she covered her face, bursting into tears as Carol screamed almost to shatter the glass around us.

"Megan took her life years ago, honey." He cried. "We kept it secret from you both. We didn't want to cause you that much pain,"

"You're lying! She would never do that!" She screamed. My dad looked up at Carol as her body fell backwards and slammed into the chair. My mom came to me, wiped the tears off my face, and walked me to my room,

"Come, sweetie," she said. "Daddy needs to talk to Carol now," she said in a soft voice. And as I began walking to my room, I turned to Carol.

That bright light that once surrounded her began to dim as if the sunshine was sucked right out of her soul. Once glowing with hope, her face became grim, and with that grim, her illusions, hopes, and dreams came crashing down.

There was no freedom. There was no better life. There was no Europe after all.

Those free birds weren't birds anymore. They turned to stone in the middle of chaos.

CHAPTER 29

"She isn't safe?" Dread gathers around my throat and chokes me. My face is hot, and my body feels weak. I can't think clearly. Just picturing Carol in danger makes me cringe. Goosebumps have circled around my skin, and I shake my hands. "No," I tell myself. "She is ok. She is fine,"

Jack changes his tone of voice right away, but he tells me Derek never kept his word with girls.

Plural. There were many girls, according to Jack.

He says Derek ran from house to house, playing three little pigs.

"Three little pigs?"

"Yeah, you know the story…."

"Yeah, but I don't get it."

"Keeps going from house to house to see which house, or girl, crumbles first,"

If he's right, I knew it. I felt it.

There was something weird going on with him. All of his secrecy and how he treated Carol. The manipulation! And Carol fell for it!

Who wouldn't fall for a tall, dark, handsome man with green eyes? My sister did! And she kept secrets for him.

No, that's not possible. She is smart! That can't be!

"I don't believe you," My voice cracks.

"Hey, maybe I'm wrong with your sister," he says.

What if I am wrong? What if she is in danger?

If he was using Carol, where is she now? In a room like me? Or worse? And who's fault is it?

Mine! I kept her life a secret! I was an accomplice to her decisions. If I just had spoken up, she would be home. I would be home, and we would be ok.

I try to focus my attention on the road, trying to clear my head when I see French Camp Road once again.

"Jack…"

He sighs.

"Can we…"

"No," He interrupts me.

"Please. I haven't seen my parents. I don't know if

they're ok. Just for a little bit. I promise I will return for whatever you need me,"

Jack lowers his head and stares into his phone. He shakes his head, telling me that it's a no.

"We have to go back to the house now," I reach for his arm, and he confusingly stares at it. Like I did something horrible by touching him.

"Just to check on my parents. Please," He looks at me and then back at the road. He sighs, and I know. He is going to take me home.

He moves his arm quickly away from mine and grabs the steering wheel, but I smile at him. I don't care. After three months or so, I am finally going to see my parents.

We get off the freeway and turn the corner. My car is missing! The convenience store is boarded up with plywood, and the city that once was minimally active is now an abandoned ghost town.

They've evacuated.

The liquor store has 2x4s across the doors, and the windows are shattered.

What the hell happened?

"Take a right on Boulder," I say. "There it is!"

He drives past the front yard, and I see the lamp

by the window—Jack parks on the corner, two houses down from mine and sighs. I can tell he is annoyed.

"Jack, I am going to help you with what you need from me. I am coming back,"

"That's not it," he says, bothered.

I get off the truck, and he gets off with me. He pulls a gun from the glove compartment and looks around.

"This shit feels weird," he says as I keep walking.

"It's always like that," I say as he shakes his head.

"No, it's not,"

My dad's fences are fallen over. The chain-link wall is torn, and the back door is broken.

"What the…"

"I told you," he said, "You guys live like this?"

"It wasn't…." I run to the back door, but Jack grabs my hand and holds me back.

"No, don't do that. What if someone is in there?"

"Yeah, my parents,"

"Would your parents live like this?" He says as I stare at the broken windows. No. They wouldn't.

"Stay here," he says.

He walks in cautiously, and within a few minutes, Jack comes out. "No one is here," he says.

"What? My parents never leave!" I run inside the house.

This isn't my home!

It smells like it's been abandoned for years. The plates are left unclean, the stove is missing, and a cup of coffee is served on the kitchen table with dust around it.

"No," I cry. "They never leave! They wouldn't leave without me!" I cry.

Jack sighs. His face tells me something more. "Kate, I'm sorry. They're not here," he says as I walk around the living room.

And with every step, a broken heart. I walk into my room. To my surprise, this is worse than the rest of the house. Shattered windows, broken drawers, and trash scattered everywhere. Everything has been turned over. My clothes are missing from the closet and even my books are missing.

Why are they missing if the living room stuff is still there? Jack walks behind me and looks around.

"Oh, shit,"

"What?"

"Someone came in here."

"What do you mean?"

"This room has been ransacked. Look," He points

to a wire on the wall and then kicks over a cabinet to expose more wires.

"We have to go," he says as he pulls me. "We have to go now!" he says.

He pulls me out and as we walk back, we hear a car in the front of the house. "Fuck!" Jack shouts and drops to the floor, pulling me down with him. We crawl right beside the siding as someone enters and walks around.

He pulls me in between the house and bushes and covers my mouth.

"There's nothing here, man!"

"But that thing beeped!"

"That shit is useless!"

"We never cover the damn windows,"

"We need Jack's shit, man. Then, we'll have some good stuff," he says.

They go away but Jack remains where he is until the car is at a distance. He then pushes me away and dusts himself off. The look he usually has; mad again.

Back to angry.

He doesn't anything and I don't want to say anything else. The best thing for me is to shut up right now.

That's not my main thought, though.

Where are my parents?

Where is Carol?

And why did they leave without me?

I look down and notice a wallet on the floor.

I pick it up and flip it over.

What the fuck?

My eyes grow wide, and I can't believe what I'm seeing. This is Jack's wallet? Why does he have a picture of himself and two kids? Why are they holding an "I Love You, Daddy" sign?

What the fuck?!

What the holy hell?!

He has kids?!

Jack yanks the wallet away from my hand and quickly puts it in his pocket.

Oh, my God!

I freeze for a moment, staring at the floor, motionless. I want to ask a lot of things, but I can't. I can't bring myself to ask.

How could that be? Where are they? Who is the mother? Is Lisa the mother? Did she take them away?

We walk back to the truck in silence.

He cautiously drives, but he notices me staring. And when he catches me, I look away like a dumbass. I can't stop thinking about it.

What happened?

There are endless ways to answer this question, but I want to know! I want to know more.

I bite my lip from asking.

Should I even dare?

I have to. I want to know.

"Jack..." I say.

"Now is not the time, Kate. No questions."

And like always, like vomit spewing from my mouth,

"Where are your children?"

CHAPTER 30

Jack slams his foot on the brakes, and I slam forward into the dashboard, screaming. The truck skids and slides to a complete stop and I stare at him when I notice his knuckles turning white as he grips the steering wheel.

Then, in a violently maneuver, he kicks the door open and walks around the hood towards my side.

"Jack, stop!" I scream.

He pulls my door open, but I pull it closed right away. I tug on it as Jack punches the door and pulls it open again. He grabs my arm and pulls me out aggressively.

He then slams my body against it.

"Jack!"

"Shut the fuck up!"

"Stop!"

"You understand what it means to shut the fuck up?!"

"I was just asking!"

"Don't ask anything! Just shut up!"

"How did they get to my house, then?"

"What?"

"Them, the men! Why would they go to my house?"

"What are you talking about?"

"Why did they mention you at *my* house?"

He stays quiet and looks to the side, like wondering the same thing, like this thought never crossed his mind.

"Son of a bitch," he says as he rushes to the driver's side.

"Get in!" He takes off and we drive. He drives like a maniac. I've never seen anyone drive like this.

We arrive at his house and he storms inside. The first thing he does is walk downstairs into the basement. I don't want to go down there again but he comes back and walks into the kitchen, where two guys are eating.

"Who's been down there?" He shouts

"What are you talking about?"

"Someone's fucking with me! Who's been down there?"

"No one, Jack."

"That's bullshit!"

"No, I swear…."

"The only person allowed down there is Eric! Where is he?"

"I don't know,"

And out of the blue, one of them points at me.

"What about her? She's been here for a little while, and she's been down there with Eric!" I stare at Jack, who turns to me, and then I look back at the guy, angry at the accusation.

"It's not by choice! You are the one that brought women in here!" I pointed back and his mouth drops,

"And you were the one talking to them!" The guy yells back. Jack turns to me and squints.

His look says it all.

"What does he mean, talking to them? Who were you talking to?" I take a step back, but he shadows my movement.

"The girls. The ones he invited over," I say.

"What does he mean talking to them? What did you say to them?" Oh no…

"They- they asked me if I was invited to the party, and I said no."

"What *did* you tell them?"

"I told them you wanted me here,"

Jack places his hand on his forehead and signals the guys to go away with his finger.

"That doesn't matter, though. I didn't touch your machine, Jack." He walks downstairs into the basement, and I go to him. He reaches from the back and pulls the wires from behind.

Sparks fly out of the back, and I flinch as the computer screens turn bright white just before shutting down.

"Jack, I didn't know I couldn't say anything. I was just making small talk. I wasn't sure how to respond. What could I do? They asked!"

"You could have shut the fuck up!" he slams his fists on the table enough to rattle everything on it.

"That's just basic shit you need to learn here. This isn't a fucking motel! That's just fucking common sense!"

"I know! But you have no idea how bored I was!"

"That doesn't matter,"

"I didn't touch your machine,"

"I know you didn't," he sighs.

"Then why are you mad at me?"

"Because you told a fucking girl that I wanted you here!" he says disappointedly.

"And?"

"You don't say shit like that to anyone! Now because of that, they're gonna be looking for you, too!"

"Who?"

"The people who are looking for me!"

"What are they looking for?"

"Stop asking questions!"

"No! Not when they're at my house! Not when I'm in danger for it! Not when they could know where Carol is!"

"They don't know where your sister is…" he sighs.

"They might!"

"No, they don't."

"They might!"

"You say your sister left with Derek, right?"

"Yea,"

"Well, your sister is probably dead now,"

"You are such an asshole!" I scream as I rush upstairs. I push the door open and walk towards my room as I hear Jack laughing behind me. I shut the door and lock it.

I don't want to think of that. I don't want to think of Carol being dead. Jack knows how to piss me off. He knows what my worst fear is, and he is using it against me.

And he wins again.

I hate that feeling.

I cover my mouth as I want to cry.

I try to stop but I can't. I can't even try.

"Kate," Jack says, moving the doorknob, "Open it," He laughs.

"No,"

"Open the door,"

"Go away,"

"Listen, I don't feel like buying another bedroom door, but I will if I have to,"

I open the door and he stands by it.

"What do you want from me, Jack?"

"I want you to listen."

"Why me? Why do you have me here?"

"I'm not going to start that again."

"Jack," I start crying. "Just leave me alone."

My hope crumbles.

I've wanted to hold onto a bit of hope since I came here, but Jack is right. Carol never made it to Europe.

My parents are nowhere around, and I'm stuck inside a house with nowhere to go.

I have nowhere to go!

He is right. Everyone is right. I am alone.

Jack comes over and sits next to me.

"Oh my God, they're all gone!" I cry.

"Listen," he sighs. "Your parents are probably ok. I didn't see any blood in the house so that's a good sign. I can't find Derek, which means he probably got away. Your sister is probably with him, which means she is probably safe."

"I would believe you if you didn't say, Probably, so much," He smiles.

He stays quiet for a moment and then places his hand on my thigh.

"I'm a jerk. I'm sorry." He smiles and stands up. "I'll leave you alone. You've had enough of my bullshit today."

He walks to the door, and I call his name.

"Dear fucking Lord, it's the most I've heard my name since I was born. What?"

"You would tell me if you heard anything about Carol, right?"

"What do you mean,"

"I don't know. If you found Derek, you would tell me about her if she was around?"

"Yeah,"

"Thank you,"

"Don't thank me. I'm the one who has you here...."

"True. But because of Carol, I probably would have been dead anyway...."

"Probably," Jack says as he closes the door behind him.

CHAPTER 31

For the past two weeks, Jack is the one bringing me lunch and dinner. I think today is another rendition of simple peanut butter and jelly sandwich with a cup of milk.

I don't mind it, though.

Food in my position is a constant battle between forcing it down my throat and throwing it up. I still find living here hard to swallow even though Jack seems to have cooled off of me.

Today in the morning, he brought me an iPod. A classic device to play music. I was a little hesitant about using it, but he assured me these things are far from a computer. "Your medieval mind can calm down," he said.

He added songs to which I am very fond of. I've always loved music. But after dad took that away, we were left with books. Little did he know that books sparked more of an imagination in me than music did.

I just think he feared Carol finding inspiration from music as much as Aunt Megan did so I can't blame him.

Jack finds it hard to believe that we lived as we did. He pokes fun of my "Amish" ways. We were far from it, though. My dad would have loved that idea.

If my dad would only see this iPod and its music, he would be twitching.

Jack has an interesting take on music. I am much closer in my research to go ahead and diagnose him with Bipolar tendencies. His music does confuse me, though. Some music is beautiful: calm, serene, soft intros, and endings.

Others? Well, others are angry and gloomy. They do give me a hell of emotions, though. Some emotions I've never felt before. Some make me want to dance. Others make me want to throw myself under the blanket and crumble. I totally understand his mood changes now.

"You're still on that thing?" Jack says as he enters.

"It has so much,"

He smiles and hands me my plate. He sits on the sofa and watches as I eat. Oh yes, he stays here too. I just think he feels bad because he knows I have nowhere to go anymore. I think he felt bad when I told him I wanted to be alone. I'm sure he has better things to do, but I do enjoy his company.

He's funny sometimes. I prefer funny Jack instead of the beast hiding underneath- a monster riddled with anger issues and alcoholic drinks. Actually, I don't think I've ever seen him drink anything else. "I've never see you eat," I say.

"I eat,"

"You drink a lot, though,"

"It's not that bad,"

"No?"

"No."

"When do you eat?"

"I'm not here twenty-four-seven, am I?"

"I am."

He stays quiet for a moment, "I know you are bored."

"Well, you are too,"

"How?"

"Well, you're here twice a day. That has to mean that either one, you are bored and have nothing to do. Or two, I am the pig being fed before the feast,"

He laughs.

"I'm here for my amusement. You're fucking nuts!"

His phone rings, and he answers. His face becomes serious as he walks to the window, then he hangs up and looks at his watch.

"Paranoid, much?"

He smiles. "I have to watch out."

"I wouldn't be so calm knowing people were looking for me,"

"You aren't calm anyway,"

"If I had a gun, I would carry that with me at all times."

"Yes, we've all seen your desperate attempts to shoot me. However, I think I need to teach you basic survival skills. You're a Bambi walking in a desert storm,"

"You're a jackass," I laugh.

"My name is Johnny Knoxville, and welcome to Jackass," he says in a weird voice.

"Who?"

"Dear lord woman… watch some fucking TV."

He sits down, looks at his phone, and pulls his hair back. He's nervous. I have never seen him bite his nails.

"You're not as relaxed as other days,"

"Two weeks and you have me figured out, huh?"

"No," I add. "But you seem tense,"

He leans forward, takes the sandwich off my hand, and takes a bite. Then, he makes an ugly face.

"What?"

"The cyanide tastes disgusting," He smiles, but the joke scares me, and my smile disappears.

"Relax," He laughs.

"You would."

"I would what,"

"Do that,"

"I would?"

"I don't know…."

"I said I wasn't going to hurt you, didn't I?"

"I have to believe you?"

"Nope, but it seems you are out of a sister, home, and or parents. So, you must stay here. You gotta trust me now,"

Shit, he's right.

Even if he granted me all my wishes, I have nowhere to go. Back home? With the shattered windows? Living by myself?

Jack is right. This scares me the most. I have to stay until I figure out what I am going to do.

"Hey," Jack places his hand on my shoulder. "I made a terrible joke," he says.

"You're right, though," I say as he looks around and leans back on the sofa.

"So, you want a TV in here? It's pretty fucking boring."

"I'm ok,"

"Let me make it better. What do you want?"

"Freedom,"

"A bookshelf?"

"I said…"

"I can get a shit ton of books in here,"

"I want to go out, Jack."

He sighs. "It's not that simple."

"Why do you have me here?"

"Painting. That would be good for you,"

"Jack,"

"Maybe sculpting. I can get some supplies,"

"Jack…"

"I don't know much of watercolors, but…."

"Jack!"

"What?"

I stare.

"You can't leave…."

"Then it is all useless to me."

"Then useless it is…." He lifts abruptly, pushing the sofa back a bit. He checks for his keys and his lips press in a fine line.

"Why did that bother you?"

"Because I am trying to help you, and you get all dramatic on me,"

"I just want to go home. How is that bad?"

"You have no home to go to,"

"Ok, but out. At least out,"

"Just take what I give you for now,"

"Fine. Bring me more music," I say annoyingly.

"Music it is,"

CHAPTER 32

I have a song on repeat.

It keeps playing in my head even when it is over. It resonates with me. The song is about a man driving on a highway. He suddenly sees a bright light and a hotel. Inside, he finds a beautiful woman waiting for him at the entrance and everything is bliss. He's offered luxury and symphony, but when he wants to leave, he can't.

The man runs for the door. A desperate attempt. He then realizes his mistake, and he finds no exit. He wants to be where he was before, but someone tells him he can never leave.

An illusion of a beautiful place turned sour. He is stuck without reason.

This is my life.

This is me.

This house is my Hotel California.

"Dinner is served." Jack says with a British accent as he walks in. He hands me the plate and sits.

"No usual sandwich? Oh? And Orange juice? I must be doing good,"

"Gold star," He smiles. "What you up to?"

I wave the iPod.

"Nice," He takes the iPod off my hand.

"Why do you have Hotel California on repeat?"

"I love that song,"

"Eagles is ok,"

"It's been on repeat for hours,"

"Really? This song?"

"Yeah, why?"

"Kind of overplayed,"

"Well, it's new to me. It really speaks to me,"

"How?"

"Well, look at what he is saying. There is this man stuck inside a hotel. He can't leave. Kinda creepy,"

"Uh-huh," he notices I'm comparing this situation to the song. "He's stuck," I say.

"How does that speak to you?" he squints.

"You don't know?"

"I do. I just want you to say it,"

"I can't leave this place."

He purses his lips. "So," he says with a pause "that makes me the Beast?"

I smile.

"That's fucked up," he laughs.

"Isn't it true?"

"That I'm the beast?"

"No, but the symbolism is spot on, don't you think?"

"You forget one thing, though,"

"What?"

He sings, "But they just can't kill the beast!"

"I didn't mean to call you a beast,"

"It's all right. I've been called worse…."

"But…"

"*But* even though that is a good song, there are far better ones out there. You should listen to Led Zeppelin. Here," he says as he pulls his phone out and puts on a song. And after a bit, he shifts in his seat and sighs.

What?" I ask.

"This is just boring,"

"I'm getting used to it,"

"You sure you don't want a TV in here?"

I shake my head.

"Come on. The day would go much faster if you did,"

I wave the iPod, and he rolls his eyes. He stays a bit but then convinces me to go to his room and I do. We walk in and he immediately serves us drinks.

"We're watching TV tonight," he says as he gets himself comfortable on the sofa and throws a pillow at me.

"Are you ever going to let me go?" I ask.

"I guess, someday."

"I miss having a life,"

"You called that having a life? You don't even know what Jackass was. A kid your age would love Jackass," he smiles.

"I'm twenty-five."

He rolls his eyes. "Sorry, I meant you old people,"

I grab the blanket and sit beside him. He glances at me and looks at me confused. I am sure he is confused as to why I sat so close to him, but I don't care. He doesn't scare me anymore. And as he points the control to the TV, I stare at his arms. And he catches me staring.

"What?"

"You have tons of tattoos,"

"Yup," He drinks, "Got most of them in jail,"

"Jail?"

"Yup,"

"How was that like?"

"I dunno, you tell me," He laughs. "I'm kidding," I shake my head, but I smile.

"Why were you in jail?"

"Stupid. I got myself caught,"

"Doing?"

He shakes his head, knowing that questions are coming.

"Just dumb stuff. Can we play twenty questions another day?"

I got it. I'll leave my annoyance for another day. I lay back and place my head on the sofa and we watch TV for some time. And he is right yet again. Time flies watching TV but as the shows keep going, Jack keeps pouring one drink after another. That bottle of alcohol is almost empty, and he doesn't even pour that much soda into it.

It's not 50/50. He must be wasted.

"You drink a lot, don't you?" He looks at me and sighs.

"Twenty questions?"

I roll my eyes and stay quiet.

"It's ok," he says.

He stands up, places the cup on the counter, and walks to the door.

"You want to get out of here?" He asks. Oops. He got bothered by my questions. Time to go, I guess. I walk past him without saying a word.

"You didn't answer me,"

"You told me to get out,"

"Out of the house…."

"Oh, I thought you were telling me to get out of the room,"

"No. Out. Out of this house for a couple of days,"

"Oh, yeah, I would love that!"

"Get your shit ready. We're leaving tomorrow morning,"

And as I walk, he doesn't follow me. He closes his door, and he leaves me be.

What is going on?

Nevertheless, I rush to the room, almost running. I frantically look for a bag to put my shirt and jeans in. I look around and grab my toothbrush and a sweater. Where are we going?

Oh! I am excited and nervous.

He said for a couple of days, too!

Shit, I can't sleep!

I keep tossing and turning, staring at the clock

beside the bed. Time sure runs slow when you anticipate something. I hate this feeling. I notice the morning shine and I stare at the door and around eight, Jack knocks.

"Kate," he calls as I jump up right away.

Eric approaches us before walking out and Jack hands him his cellphone and some other things. Eric looks at me a little worried but doesn't say anything else, and I begin to get a little nervous.

He's nervous because he knows Jack and his temper. I am nervous for it too, but weirdly, I am more excited.

"You look happy," Jack says as we jump inside the truck and he's right. I am.

We drive onto the freeway, and I notice we are going south. I lay my head on the window, and my eyes become heavy.

"Go to sleep. I'll wake you up when we get there," Jack says.

And I listen.

Why do I listen?

A little while ago, I compared him to a beast. A monstrous creature who has kept me locked up for months. And now, I was excited to be out of his house, with him?

Oh, no Kate. What are you doing?

CHAPTER 33

My head jolts as the truck drives through an unpaved road. We drive deeper into the mountains where enormous trees shine bright red. They must be twenty feet wide.

A beautiful painting becomes reality and I find myself in awe. I didn't know California was this beautiful. This is a picture snapped right out of a dream.

Jack arrives at a cabin behind a tree. The house is small and looks cozy. He walks to the house and walks outside a few moments later.

"Good!" he shouts from the door, and I grab my bag and his backpack. God, the aroma of fresh pine is sensational. This is breathtakingly beautiful. The walls are made of wood instead of concrete, the kitchen is gorgeous, and a small dining room is covered with deer heads.

Jack takes his backpack and lays it beside the TV

by the fireplace. He walks into the bedroom, and I sit on the couch.

"Aren't you going to put your scraps in the bedroom?"

"Scraps?"

"Yeah, those things," He points to my bag.

"Well, buy me clothes then,"

He laughs, "Here," He tosses over a t-shirt, and it lands on my shoulder,

"Really?" He laughs again.

"Well, I'm taking a shower," he shouts. And through the open door, he lifts his arms, and with that, off comes his T-shirt. I try not to look but I am looking.

And when he turns to pick up his towel, I notice a burn scar across his ribcage, above his hip bone. He catches me, and I awkwardly look away but not without catching him smiling back at me.

"Jack?"

"No." he quickly responds.

"What? I haven't asked anything,"

"I'm not telling you about my scar."

Ok, he got me. I am not asking.

Yet.

I stand to look outside, and I still can't believe I

am here. This is all so stunning. It almost makes me forget where I am. I don't know how long I stood here because Jack comes in and stands behind me and peeks through. Freshly showered.

"Beautiful, isn't it?" He says as he walks into the kitchen and pulls a bottle from the cupboard. He walks over and sits on the sofa, shirtless. And my eyes lock to his chest. His scar is big. It looks fresh and leathery as if it is brand new. But his chest tattoos really cover it nicely.

"Stop it," He mumbles without looking at me.

"What?" I ask as he turns on the TV. I try to distract myself by looking outside again.

"Those trees have to be genetically grown,"

"No… They're naturally like that,", he says chuckling at my comment. He stands up, pulls a few things out of his backpack, and gives me a lunch bag. He places the bottle of alcohol next to his plate and pours himself yet another drink.

"So, you always have a drink in hand?"

Jack sighs.

"Have you ever been sober?"

Silence.

"I don't drink much. Never was a party person, really…" He glances at me then back at the TV.

"You like to be alone, don't you?" He clears his throat.

"That's ok. I've always been alone too. I mean, besides my sister. She was the only person I confided in," I say.

And then, the news comes on:

"The people and the city of Sacramento can begin building a safer city for its citizens. However, most women and representatives are concerned if the rate of missing women might lessen or worsen as the city begins rebuilding what was once a freedom society."

"Jack?" He sips his glass and shifts his eyes towards me.

"How was life before all of this?"

"Kate,"

"I'm not asking about your own life, just in general,"

"I'm not that old," He smiles.

"I know, but I think you know more than I do."

"What year were you born?"

"2045," I say.

He places his drink down and lowers the TV volume.

"Well, my dad began locking us up since I can remember. I think he did that right after my mom got pregnant. Or maybe it was when my grandpa lost everything, I'm not sure,"

"So, you were born in a cage…."

"Pretty much, but it kept me safe for a while,"

"And your sister?"

"She hated it. That's why we began sneaking out,"

"That doesn't sound safe at all,"

"Well, I tagged along for my sister's sake. I wanted to keep her safe,"

He nods.

"When were you born?" I ask.

"2037. Great time for business. Everything was done online. Business, school. Everything."

"My dad said that eventually, everything collapsed,"

"Well, when you give that much power to the government and voluntarily put that much information online, it is bound to."

"What do you mean?"

"Well, personal information is worth more than a bar of gold. And when that is easily attainable, you have access to bank accounts, social security numbers and shit,"

I look at the TV: Pictures of cities around the US flash across the screen. People are living in abandoned buildings; people are boarding up burnt-up houses and living on the street.

"So, where are you in all of this?"

"What do you mean?"

"Well, don't you guys do stuff like that?"

"Like what?"

"I dunno," He smiles.

"I'm good with technology, and I like easy money,"

"So?"

"Not always a good combination,"

"How?"

"I was young when I started working at Google. I screwed a lot of people and got myself into a shit load of trouble,"

I get caught on his face. His expression. His aloofness on screwing people over. If I were him, I would be terrified. And here he is, casually talking about jail. I couldn't even show a person a receipt without thinking they would find me. The gut it takes for someone to do what he does is beyond me. "What?" He says as he notices my daze.

"Does Europe have the technology, and do they have the same issue as here?"

"You mean, crime?"

"Yeah…"

"They do. Crime is everywhere," he says. "They have it under control, though. People unite and follow regulations. That's how it should work, but the US doesn't understand,"

"Have they ever?"

"Well, England tried to help us, but after a couple Englishmen were murdered in New York city, they decided to stand back."

"You ever plan to leave to Europe?"

"Nope,"

"Why?"

"Because I'm probably going to die here."

"Don't say that"

"Shh…"

"No, really…"

"No, shut up, hold on…."

"What?"

"Stay here."

He rushes to the window, opens the curtain slightly, and peeks out. He points towards the bedroom, directing me to go to it. I head to the room, and Jack follows. He walks behind the back door and pushes a small opening. He squeezes us into the aperture, a small room enough for one person, but he keeps me pressed against the wall with his chest.

"Be quiet…" he whispers.

Footsteps outside.

My chest tightens, and I feel I am out of air. I start breathing a little faster, but Jack looks down at me. He shakes his head and knows I am about to scream but he grabs a hold of me. My throat scratches and he places his hand over my mouth and puts my head against his chest.

The footsteps come into the room, and he holds his breath. Someone is here. Then, the backdoor slams into our crevice, and I jump. Jack lifts his finger to shush me, and after a few minutes, there is silence again.

The sound of tires crunching the leaves makes me feel better and Jack whispers that he will step out.

Suddenly, four gunshots. I scream, but he keeps covering my mouth and tells me everything is ok. He thinks they just blew the tires.

"I am going to check. Stay here and stay quiet," he whispers. A few minutes later, I hear Jack shouting. He comes into the room and stomps around.

He is looking for something.

Oh no!

He found my plastic bag.

The bag crumples, and he hits the wall.

"Get out, Kate!"

"No, Jack! Let me explain," I say as I push the crevice open. And as I see the gun, I shriek. He forcefully grabs my hand and tugs me. He tosses the black tracking box in front of me. The one I took from under his seat the day we went to the river.

"What the fuck is this?" He says as he walks around the room.

"Let me explain…."

"You're not answering fast enough!"

He pulls me into the bathroom and lets me go as he turns the water on. I stare at him, confused with my back against the door. He sits by the toilet as he holds his head in his hands. His ears are red.

"Jack, listen…" He launches at me, and I scream. He grabs my neck and pulls me as I hit the cabinet with my body. "Please, stop!" I shout but he doesn't.

"Who made contact with you?"

"What?!"

Jack grabs the tracking box and drops it on the floor. He lifts his foot and slams it on the box, cracking it instantly while I launch to it to save it.

"No!" I pick up a few broken pieces, hoping the

main ones are saved, but they're not. He grabs the gun and arms it and I raise my hands over my head.

"Jack, please!" I scream as I kneel in front of him. "No, Jack! I didn't bring anybody here! I didn't make any contact!"

With one pull, he grabs me by my t-shirt and drops my head into the water, pushing me in all the way. I try to scream, but water comes in through my mouth and my nose. I try to pull away, but I am not able to. His hand is holding me underwater.

I am going to drown!

Dear God, I am going to die!

"Who made contact with you!" he shouts as he pulls me out. "No one! Stop!" I shout as he dunks me once again. With a free hand, I pull his. I hit his hand enough for him to pull back. "Jack! Let me talk, please!" I cry.

Jack lets me go and leans back. He stays quiet, waiting for me to talk and he stares into my eyes, but I have nothing to say. He doesn't move. He doesn't take his stare off of me.

What am I going to say?

That I wanted the box to track or contact Derek?

That I wanted Derek to find me so I can then find Carol? That I took the tracking box and pushed all the buttons to see if someone could contact me?

He isn't going to believe me!

I launch for the door, but he grabs me by my waist, and I slide back into the bathroom. "I don't want to hurt you, but I fucking will if you don't talk!" He shouts.

"Ok," I cry, "Ok. I didn't do anything wrong,"

An angry laugh. He reaches for the gun, but I grab hold of his hand.

"No!" I yell. He lifts his eyebrows, waiting for me to say more. "But I did steal the box,"

"Why?"

"That's the only way I can have any connection to Carol. I- I wanted to see if anyone would contact us. Maybe then, I could find her." I say.

He lets me go. "It's true, Jack. Please, you have to believe me." I cry.

Jack walks out and slams the bedroom door shut. He doesn't come back. He leaves me alone, sitting in the bathroom. And I stare at the black box. The only connection I had to Carol was lying in front of me, shattered into broken pieces.

CHAPTER 34

"I'm going to Europe!" Carol said the last time I saw her. It had been ten days since we heard about Aunt Megan, and Carol was already planning her trip to Europe. These were the first words she said to me after the night my dad caught us.

Dad separated our rooms. Mine became the farthest back, and Carol was right beside my parents. I guess they were trying to keep an eye on her, but she found a way every night to sneak out.

Carol and I grew apart pretty fast.

We grew more apart in those ten days than in our entire life. She closed herself off. For the first few days, I heard her crying. She didn't come out to eat unless we took food to her.

All I wanted was to help her, but she didn't want to talk to any of us. And at night, I would often catch her climbing the fence and leave in a striped brown car. And every time, my mom would come in crying, asking me if I knew who was inside that car.

Mom said it. She predicted Carol never to come back. And it was Carol's goal not to.

"What are you talking about?"

"Derek! He is taking me to Europe!"

"You're crazy, Carol!"

"We are going down to San Francisco! He says some airplanes or boats can take us there!"

"You're not serious!"

"You think I want to stay here?"

"I thought you said you were done with him!"

"Kate, he apologized! We're ok now."

"I don't know…."

"Be happy for me, please. You'll be the only one."

She ran to her room and came back with her luggage. It took almost all my energy not to scream. I was afraid for her. I tried to take away her luggage but she stopped me right away.

"You're leaving now?!"

"Shh!" She covered my mouth and stared at the back door, hoping that mom or dad wouldn't hear us.

"I have to! We need to get ready!" She said, walking towards my back window. "Here," She handed me a cell phone. "We can communicate through this,"

"Oh, no! I don't want that!" I said while I pushed the phone away from me. The little silver cellphone freaked me out even more. I wanted nothing to do with it. Those things were going to get me or her killed.

"Kate, come on! Please! I'll call you once I'm in San Francisco. After that, just toss it anywhere in the city," I stared at the phone and then looked at her.

"Ok, fine, but I'll toss it just after you call me," I said, putting the phone away in the drawer. She smiled and hugged me. This is what she wanted, and she was going to try until she died. I couldn't stop her, let alone convince her to think otherwise. Her face was bright. That smile could not be wiped out with anything.

"I love you, little sis," She cried.

"Carol…" My voice cracked. "I'm going to be ok," she said. "You understand me, right?"

"Please call me," I said as she began climbing out, "And then toss it," She added. She ran and climbed inside the car.

And I cried all night. I was left speechless. I wish I could have told her more things. But there was no time left. And I had just another rule to follow. Talk to her one last time, and then toss it.

Yeah, I can do that, I thought.

CHAPTER 35

Another failed lead to Carol. Just when I feel I am making progress, it shatters in front of my eyes. I push the broken pieces away as I sit inside the bathroom.

Jack doesn't return; he knows I fucked up enough, but I am trying to find my sister.

What else can I do? I don't know how these things work, but some things are bound to come through. If Jack knows Derek, then I have something on Carol. And I will have to keep trying.

"You have no idea how safe you are with me. The least fucking thing you can do is listen," Jack says as I enter the living room.

"Excuse me?"

"Yea,"

"What?"

"You would be dead if it weren't for me,"

"What are you talking about?"

"I saved you,"

"You call this saved?"

"Yes," he puts out his cigarette and leans back with his hands behind his head. "Well, if it weren't for me, they would have killed you by now." he adds.

"Well, you are halfway there."

"I'm brutal, but them? They're insane,"

"You're a dick, Jack...."

"Look at it this way. You would have died at home anyway,"

"I was fine at my house,"

"I saw what I saw. They had wires on your house. They ransacked the shit out of your room. If you were there, they would've got you. And here you are bitching over little tugs,"

"Little tugs...?"

"I don't know! But I saved you...."

"It was your stupid little party girlfriends who did that! If I weren't in your house, they would have never known who the hell I was...."

"Hey, hey, hey... watch it. Your stupid little sister was one of those party girls." I walk up and smack the drink out of his hand, and it falls on him. He stares at the glass on the floor and dusts his pants. He stares blankly at the floor and smiles. He shakes his head from side to side and leans back, wiping himself with a pillow.

And I stand in front of the TV, burning from the inside. He leans sideways and grabs the bottle to serve himself another drink. He sips it, places it on the coffee table, and removes his T-shirt.

"Can you move? I can barely see the TV,"

Shit.

My lip trembles.

Stop it, no crying. I yell inside my head.

I am not sure if these tears are from anger or sadness, but I am crying profusely. Jack looks up at me and moves me aside with his arm.

"Take the bedroom. The guys are going to bring me a truck tomorrow," I wipe my eyes and start heading for the room. "I asked the guys to check on us just in case someone comes back. No need to ask your twenty questions," he adds and I slam the door shut. It echoes throughout the cabin and I hear him laughing.

Carol was that party girl. She was precisely those girls. My stomach hurts knowing she was part of all this. The things she must have seen or heard about.

And the worst part is that she was perfectly ok with that.

I keep tossing and turning.

I can't sleep.

Every few minutes or so, I keep looking outside, hoping the sunrise comes so I don't have to force my eyes shut.

I nod off for a few minutes when I see the bathroom light on. I stand up as quietly as I can and notice the door is cracked open just a bit. Jack is standing by the mirror, leaning over the sink. I thought he was brushing his teeth for a moment, but instead, he is in pain.

He splashes his face with water and lowers his head. He stretches up and pulls his hair back, but then he flinches like something stabbed his chest.

Then, he pulls a prescription bottle from a zip lock bag under the sink. A handful of pills fall into his palm, and he takes them. He cups some running water and gulps them all down.

All of them. A lot of them.

But then he stares into the mirror for a few seconds, and for a brief moment, I see him weaker than he seems to be. I get the way he is.

His abuse, his words, his anger. Just as kids lash out at their parents, Jack lashes out at the world. And he does a good job hiding behind all the alcohol bottles and apparently, the pills.

His eyes are dark. He hurts. I know he does. He turns the water off, and I rush to the bed. I cover myself, and he walks out and into the living room.

Then, glasses again- another drink.

I slowly make my way to the door and push it open just a bit.

"You aren't very good with the spying," he mumbles. I open the door and stand by it. Did he see me in the bathroom, or does he mean right now?

"Why are you up so early?"

"Couldn't sleep. Why aren't you sleeping?"

"I wake up early every day,"

"Why?"

He gives me a bothered look. "Really? I'm not ready for this," I smile at him and walk back inside the bedroom.

"You want to see something?" He stops me.

"What do you mean?"

He walks by me into the bedroom and opens his backpack. He pulls two sweaters and hands me one. "Put this on. It's gonna be cold outside," I follow him into the trees. The dawn creates a mist through the trees, making it difficult to see beyond a few feet, but

Jack keeps walking, and I start to worry. I stand near him, and he looks at me and smiles. I'm sure he knows I'm scared, and he slows down a bit so I can catch up.

We keep walking through the bushes and a couple of trees and I admire them. The mist has now cleared a little bit enough for me to enjoy the scenery.

Oh, wow.

The morning sky is covered in stars and a gorgeous shade of blue. The sun hasn't quite come up, and the moon is glowing still.

This is unreal.

Porch lights illuminate hundreds of houses down the mountain and the blue and purple sky shines over the city, creating a breathtaking panorama.

"It is gorgeous, isn't it?" He says.

"It is. I can't take my eyes away from it,"

"Get up there," He points to a rock. "Better view," he says as he helps me up. And as I step into it, I feel a warming in my heart. A warmth I haven't felt in a while. It makes me a little sad to know we are surrounded by such beauty but blinded by the ugliness that we have.

If only I wasn't so afraid.

Jack steps back and leans into a tree to smoke a

cigarette and I look back, I need to make sure I soak everything in before going back to his house.

A rustling of birds gets my attention. I move a tree branch near, and a flock of birds fly into the horizon. My eyes water just a little bit, but I find myself screaming. But then, I step closer to the edge and open my arms wide.

"Woah!" Jack comes over and grabs me by the sweater.

"Watch it. You don't want to fall,"

"No. I want to fly," I chuckle.

"Fly?" He gives me a puzzled look.

"Yeah, birds are great! They fly wherever they want. They are beautiful little creatures who…" I stop immediately when I realize Jack is confused.

"Birds…?" He asks, making a face. I know by the lift of his eyebrow that he's convinced I'm crazy.

"Yeah. My aunt loved birds. She taught us the meaning of them,"

He crosses his arms. "The meaning?" He asks.

"Something stupid," I say right away. I sound like an idiot, but he leans sideways into a tree, waiting for me to say more.

"I have some time,"

I jump off the rock and try to act like it doesn't matter but he is giving me my time.

"Well, they're free. They have freedom. They go wherever they wish." I notice Jack making faces, and I pause, "Just something my aunt used to say, I guess."

Jack laughs and looks up at the pack of birds, "You know there are eagles and hawks out there hunting these birds, right?" I shrug my shoulders, and he adds, "Freedom comes with a price,"

"Well, at least they try to be free,"

"Wait. Are we talking about the birds or you?" He smirks. "The birds, Jack…." I say as I walk past him without waiting for him and make my way down to the cabin.

He chuckles behind me as I push branches out of the way. I speed up, just so I don't hear his dumbass laughing behind me. The moment was gone! His words keep repeating inside my head, and I am trying very hard not to turn around and throw him off that cliff.

For now, the best thing to do is go back and take a nap. Ignore it, just to remember the good moments.

My sweater gets caught on a branch, and I tug at it. I can't seem to undo it, and I yank it. And to make matters worse, I hear Jack laughing. I bite my lips, but it isn't enough, I turn around and walk to him as he stops.

"Why do you always have to be such a dick?"

"What? What did I do?" He laughs.

"Seriously,"

"What did I do?"

"Really, Jack. Those pills are doing nothing but making you delirious,"

He looks up and shakes his head.

"I see how many bottles you have and how many pills you gulp down at a time,"

"You think I take them for fun?" he smiles.

"Maybe,"

I storm into the house and walk to the bathroom. He stands by the bedroom door and stares as I grab the bag of pills he keeps under the sink.

"Don't fuck around with that," he says as I shrug my shoulders. He laughs and slams the door open while walking to the living room.

"Goddamn! All that fucking attitude just because I bring up her damn sister,"

I swing my arm and throw the bag of pills at him, but he misses it as he moves to the side. He laughs and grabs the bag and I throw myself on the bed and cover my head as he walks back into the bathroom. And then, I hear the water running again.

"More?"

"What do you mean, more?" He swings the door open.

"I saw you take a lot of pills just a few hours ago,"

He turns the water off and picks up his drink from the sink. "And alcohol doesn't help either, Jack,"

"Why the fuck do you care?" He smiles as he walks past me, but I stop him. I hold his arm and he stands there, looking at me confused as to why I did.

Why do I care? I don't have an answer for him, but I can show him.

I launch myself to him, placing my lips against his. My arms wrap around his neck, holding him against me. I kiss him with all the energy I have. I've been wanting to for a while, but he pulls back right away.

He looks at me but doesn't move. His eyes are open wide, and I lightly put my hand over my mouth, and I sigh. He doesn't respond so I slowly move aside and into the living room.

I sit on the sofa and stare at the door.

Wanting to hide, but I can't. I'm embarrassed and

nervous. I run my hands through my hair and look around to find something to do but I can't.

But I do chuckle at the absurdity.

Footsteps.

I hear Jack walking over, and I sit up.

He enters the living room and stares. He stomps towards me, and I stand up right away. I think he is going to hurt me but instead, he pushes me back and grabs my face to kiss me again.

He grabs me by my neck and pulls me in.

He sinks his lips onto mine and bites me. I run my fingers through his hair as he opens my legs. He kneels on the floor and starts running his mouth on my neck. I feel his body. It's hot, his breathing is heavy and I don't know what to do.

His hand moves down my thighs and he lifts me, pressing his body against mine. My fingertips run through his neck and then to his beard. And as my hair falls to the side, he moves it as he leans up and rests his body over mine.

I want him and he wants me too.

He grabs my butt and pulls me in and I feel him. I want him but I'm scared.

Scared and excited.

I pull his belt buckle, remove it and then he looks

down. And just like that, he rapidly lifts away from me. He leans away and breathes heavy. He runs his hand through his head and scratches it. He looks to the side and then back at me.

I am waiting for him to say something, but he doesn't. "What?" I ask.

He drags his thumb through my lips and smiles. He leans over, picks up his shirt, and walks back into the room, closing the door behind him.

A part of me was relieved.

Another part, well, I was hoping the door would reopen.

CHAPTER 36

For days after Carol left, I kept looking out the window. I had visions of that striped, brown car pulling up and Carol walking over. Regretting her decision. I wanted her to come home and live peacefully, hoping that all her hopes and dreams would be fulfilled by staying home. But that was it. Nothing but dreams.

My dad had letters ready for me to drop off in the morning. The cellphone was in my pocket, and I was hoping that it wouldn't ring as I walked through the kitchen. Dad opened the gate, and as he walked by, I saw his eyes swollen.

I knew he was probably crying. I wanted to tell them that I had a connection to her, but I didn't even know how this thing worked. "If you see her, tell her we don't want her back," he said.

"Andrew!" Mom shouted and stormed inside the

house. He followed her and shut the door, but I had to focus.

I found myself driving past the post office. I wasn't even sure where I was going. All I knew was that I needed to find her. The worry was eating me alive. I drove past every brown car. I went by every shop, every person walking and even every house near ours. People looked at me oddly. Maybe they thought I was trying to do something malicious, but I wasn't. I was just trying to find something lost.

I must have seen Carol's face in almost twenty women that day. Every woman had red hair in my eyes. Every woman was young, fair skinned and looked exactly like her. Sadly, for me, not many people were out that day.

What if I drove to San Francisco? What if I drove to the airport? After several conversations with myself, I decided to go back home.

But as I drove in, the phone rang.

I frantically opened my purse, but my dad waited by the gate. No! I can't answer! "Kate, what are you doing?" dad shouted. The phone's vibration made me nervous, and I was staring at my dad calling me over. I dropped the phone and kicked it under the seat as I saw my dad walking over.

"What the hell?" he shouts as I drove up.

The phone stopped, and I rushed outside in case it rang again. My dad walked inside, with me behind him, but the phone stayed in the car. And later that night, I rushed to it.

Oh, my God!

I didn't answer it!

Oh no, I can't toss it now!

CHAPTER 37

Finally.

Eric and Jay are here with the truck. Though, I've never seen them drive that blue truck.

"The guys are...." I stop as Jack rushes into the living room and lifts a finger to his mouth. He signals me to come over.

"Bring me my backpack..." he whispers. He opens the curtain slightly as another car pulls up, a cream-colored one and we see two men step out.

"Fuck..." Jack sighs.

"What?"

"They don't work for me," he says as I look at them walking over.

He walks to the bedroom. A loud bang goes off and the two men rush towards the trees behind the cabin. Jack runs inside and pulls me,

"Hurry the fuck up, let's go!" He says. We run to the truck, and he swings the door open. He reaches under the steering wheel, pulls wires from under the truck, and the truck starts. "What the..."

"Get in," he tells me as he pushes me to the passenger side. I look over and see both of the men running. "Fuck!" Jack shouts. "Get down!" he yells as a gunshot goes off and shatters the other car's window and I scream.

Jack floors it and we speed into the road. I turn around to look behind me but Jack yells at me to stay down so I duck. The truck swerves into the dirt path and Jack frantically searches his backpack.

"Son of a bitch, I said get down!" He shouts as he screeches into a concrete road. The men approach us, and I lift to see them right behind us. I scream as the back window shatters and then I notice Jack's arm is bleeding.

"You're hit!" I scream.

"No, I'm not! It just grazed me! Stay the fuck down!" He desperately dials and starts shouting within seconds, "Eric! I need someone to lock into me. Cream-colored Ford! Shooting! Heading west, about three miles to the 198!"

He hands me the phone as he swerves again.

"Keep this open!" He says as I grab the phone.

The car slams right, and my body with it and not without dropping the phone.

Shit!

"Son of a bitch, Kate! What the fuck did I tell you?" He yells. "Hurry the fuck up!" He shouts. "I'm trying!" I scream back. I grab the phone and open it.

And as I look up, a black car pulls next to us. "Jack, who's that?!" I shout. The window lowers, a gun comes out, and I scream.

Jack slams on the brakes, and I slam onto the dashboard as the gunshot shatters the window. I cover my face to shield it from the broken glass but Jack grabs my face to look at him.

"Are you ok?!"

"Yes!"

He speeds up again and makes a hard left onto the 198. And as soon as he hits a highway, he is able to speed away just a little further. I am somewhat relieved but terrified as I see the two cars behind us, trying to catch up.

And right away, I see two black trucks pull up next to the others. The cream car goes off the road and into the dirt, and the other one slows down.

"Finally, fuck!" he shouts.

My heart is pounding.

What the hell just happened?!

I cover my eyes and lay my head on my hands. Trying to catch a breath, I feel like I wasn't breathing for a while. My chest tightens and I cry. I clear my tears as Jack reaches for me,

"We're ok, now" he says as I look at him and notice his shirt is covered in blood. I rip a t-shirt from his backpack and lift his arm to clean the blood off his right arm. But as I lift his arm, I notice a bullet hit just below his ribcage.

"Oh no! Jack!" I shout as I push the t-shirt onto it. "Pull over!" I scream.

He pulls out of the highway and immediately stops. He holds his side and grunts. "Fuck…" He says as I look around.

I need something to help him with.

Oh, my God! What do I do?!

"We need help!" I scream and Jack hands me the cellphone. "Call Eric," he says, leaning back.

His head drops and his skin becomes pale.

"No, no, no, Jack, come on… look at me," I say as I shake his head. His eyes roll behind his head, and I panic. "Jack! Wake up, Jack!" I pull his chin towards me, and he looks at me again.

"Oh, God! How do I use this?!" I scream as I hold

his phone in my hand. But the phone rings, and I see Eric's name.

"What's going on? Where are you?" Eric shouts.

"Jack, he is hit!" I shout back.

"Ok, tell me where you are!"

"Oh my God, I don't know!"

"Ok, we're locking into you! Do not close the phone! What's going with Jack?"

"He doesn't… he's not…."

"Kate, calm down!"

"He's not listening to me. He's not responding. He's dying!"

"Ok, I need you to stay calm, though. What is Jack doing?"

"Hurry, please!"

I leave the phone on the dashboard and turn to Jack again.

"Jack!" I shout. His eyes open very little, "Ok, Ok, like that, listen to me," I say. "Wake up. Eric's coming!"

I grab the t-shirt, and I push it in as Jack shouts.

"What the fuck are you doing?!" He pushes my hand out of the way.

"Listen to me, Jack, hey," I lift his face and while I look around, he stares into my eyes. I try to move but he keeps my face intact. Like he doesn't want me to look away.

"Do me a favor," He sighs.

"Stay up, please…." I sigh.

He adjusts himself and grunts. He leans his head back and holds onto his side, and I look for Eric. I jump out of the truck and run to his side. And as I swing the door open, Eric pulls out of the freeway.

"Ok, Jack. They're here!" I yell.

Eric and Jay run to us, and they drag Jack into the other truck and I sit with him in the back seat.

"I'm fine," Jack says, laughing but in pain.

I shut the door and keep his head up. His hair falls into his face, and I move it aside.

"You ok, man?" Jay asks as Eric makes a U-turn into the highway. I look at Jay as we notice Jack's eyes rolling behind his head. Jay bites his lips and turns to Eric,

"He's gonna go, dude" he says as Eric speeds up. Eric adjusts the rearview mirror to look at Jack and then turns around, right away, to slap Jack in the face.

"What the fuck?" Jack shouts.

"Hey man, stay with us," Eric says and Jay laughs. I look at the way they aren't panicking, and I am dying here. I am terrified.

"Come on, Jack. You're cool, right? You're cool…" Jay smiles. "Turn right up ahead. That'll take you straight onto the 99," he says to Eric.

Jack sighs and looks at me.

"It's gonna get infected," I say.

"The only thing I'm worried about is that I will have to re-tattoo that side,"

"That's not funny,"

"I think I'm hilarious," he grunts. "Why didn't you take off?"

I glance over and turn to look at the road.

"Why stay here with us?" I smile but ignore him. "You had a good chance of leaving, why didn't you?"

"I thought I was the one that asked a lot of questions?"

"Hey, Jack, you alright back there?" Eric says.

"I'm fine, man," he says without taking his eyes off of me. I open his Ziploc bag filled with pills and read through them: Anti-depressants, Prozac, Zoloft, Lexapro. Painkillers, Morphine, Oxycodone, Codeine, Tramadol. And other painkillers that I can't even pronounce.

What the hell are these things?

I offer one to him, and he lifts his head to see the bag in my hand.

"Here," I say.

"I thought you hated that," he says.

"No, not when you need them," He smiles and tilts his head back again.

Eric drives off the freeway and to a hospital. They pull in front, and they drag Jack inside, but I remain behind.

Alone.

With a truck.

The streets are empty. The day is clear, and I am left alone with a truck. My temples knock the inside of my head, and I am stuck.

What do I do? Jay stands by the door and looks over. He smiles at me and walks to Eric, who then looks at me. I know what they're talking about. I can feel it. I am thinking of the same thing. But why can't I do it? I've wanted this opportunity for months, but I can't bring myself to do it. My only thought is Jack right now.

Is he going to be ok? Is he going to die?

"Anyone else would have left Jack to die," Jay says as he walks to me.

"I'm...."

"Thank you." He says.

"For?"

"To be someone who doesn't want Jack dead," he walks back, and I think: I would be halfway home by now. But I'm still confused.

I jump into the driver's seat and hold onto the steering wheel. The keys looks so nice right now. I run my fingers through the ignition and close my eyes. I turn the keys just enough to turn on the radio but not the truck entirely. It beeps, and I turn the truck back off.

Ugh. I can't go.

Not that I can't go.

Most importantly, I don't want to go.

Eric comes over as I roll down the window.

"Go,"

"What?"

"I told you I was going to help you,"

"But Jack…"

"Kate. I'm offering help,"

"Jack…"

"Jack is going to be fine…."

He pulls me in for a hug.

"I'll tell him you needed to go,"

"But he is…."

"He is going to be ok. I hope you find your sister,"

And he leaves.

He leaves me in complete control of what I want to do. But I am stuck between two worlds. I want to run, be home, have a life, and go back to normal.

I also want to know how Jack is. I want to see him get better. I want to be near him and get to know him. I want to have lunch with him and spend time together. I want to see him smile more often, and I'll like to be the person who creates that smile.

Oh, no...

I don't think I want to leave this Hotel California anymore. I think I've fallen in love with the devil.

CHAPTER 38

My mom knew something was not right, and she usually kept her thoughts to herself.

"Another nightmare, sweety?" She asked as I walked into the kitchen at 4 am. I nodded. I hadn't been able to sleep for a couple of days.

"What are you doing up?" I asked.

That's all it took to get my mom crying again. She didn't want to tell me she was waiting for Carol to come home. That she probably spends all her morning staring at her room and her nights waiting by the kitchen door.

"Mom," I sat with her for a moment. "Carol decided…" I say as she stood up and walked away. She didn't want to hear it from my mouth more so than my dad's. Carol was gone but I was going to make sure she was ok.

I opened my closet and unwrapped the towel hidden in the corner. The cellphone wasn't ringing, so I tucked it back in. One night though, it rang. I flipped that cellphone over and I held it up to my ear.

"Hello?" I whisper. Crackle.

"Hello?" I asked.

And one word was clear within all the static.

"*Sacramento*,"

Why is a man answering?! It's been breached! Someone must have gotten a hold of Carol's phone! I threw it hard over the fence.

"What's that?!" I heard dad shout as I jumped in bed. I kept quiet and still. Hoping I didn't jeopardize anything by keeping it longer than what Carol asked me to. What if Carol was with that guy? Was she trapped? What if their car broke down and they need help?

Shit!

Now, I need that thing again.

I'll go tomorrow morning to get it and hopefully, whoever called will call again. This only meant one thing to me, though. It meant that I needed to go to Sacramento now.

Ok. Sacramento, it was.

CHAPTER 39

"You're still here," Eric says.
"I know,"

"Why?"

"I don't know,"

Eric jumps on the passenger's seat and sits with me for a little bit. "Kate, Jack is not OK. And I think you know what I mean,"

"I know, but I'm not leaving this way,"

"Jack is in a fucked up place...."

"What do you mean?"

"You seem stuck between wanting to leave and wanting to stay,"

"I'm just thinking...."

"You can leave. You've wanted to all these months,"

"I will leave, but not today."

"You might not get another chance,"

"I will…"

He checks his phone and looks up at Jay, who is standing by the hospital entryway. He sends Jay a message, and Jay walks away.

"We can go see him now," he says as he leans over and takes the keys from the ignition.

The room is dim and cold. The sound of Jack's heartbeat is beeping through a machine, and I stare at the numbers on the screen as he rests his head on a pillow.

The black under his eyes is heavy, and his skin still lacks color. The gloom isn't getting better with the hospital lighting. His arm and torso are wrapped in gauze pads, and there are wires hooked up to a machine next to him. I slowly sit on the chair, but it creaks.

"Hey…"

"You don't have to talk. I just came in to see how you were,"

"I'm fine, look at me, ready to party…" he says weakly.

"Shut up," I smile.

"I'm surprised to see you here,"

"Why?"

"Thought you were gonna take off. I asked where you were, and they said you were alone outside,"

"Couldn't leave you like this,"

"Why?"

"I don't know,"

"Should have," He grunts as he adjusts himself.

"I'll leave when you feel better,"

"That's the wrong way of doing it,"

"Why?"

"Cuz' I can catch you then," He smiles. He turns, holding himself on the bar attached to the hospital bed.

"When are you getting out of here?"

"I don't know. The bullet didn't hit anything sensitive, so maybe soon,"

"Does it hurt?"

"It did,"

I glance over and stare at the prescription bottles next to the bed. "That helps, huh?" I ask.

"They do." He stares at me for a little too long.

"What?"

"I'm not kidding. If I get better, I'm not gonna let you go,"

"Yes, you will,"

"You're that confident,"

Eric enters and starts grabbing medical supplies. Jack looks at him and asks what he is doing. I look around, and Jay is talking to the hospital nurse. "Gotta go, Jack…" Eric says as Jack struggles to lift himself.

"Why? What's going on?" I ask as I help Jack out of bed.

"We just have to leave," Eric says as he looks at Jack.

"I hate this fucking hospital anyway," Jack says as we help him. We jump in the truck and Jay starts driving.

"Why do you guys hate the hospital?" I ask.

Jay turns around and hands Jack a water bottle. Jack takes a couple of pills, and Jay starts rambling.

"Well, when Jack got his scar, they didn't want to help us. Like, they made us wait for two hours before rejecting him. The only hospital that would take us was in Sacramento and by the time we got there, Jack's burn was super infected. Not only that but…"

"Hey!" Jack Interrupts. "Can you shut the fuck up already?"

Jay smiles at me, and I look at Jack.

The rest of the car ride was silent. And about an

hour in, we pull in front of his house, and a couple of guys help Jack out of the car.

Again, I was left outside, alone.

The door opens, a guy steps out and walks towards me. He grabs me by my arm and pulls me into the house. We walk upstairs and inside my room.

"What are you doing?" He sets a water bottle on the nightstand and tells me food is coming at 8 pm.

"Wait, what are you doing?" I ask again.

"If you need anything else, let us know," I shake my head and laugh, "You got this all wrong. I've been here for four months."

"I know, Kate…."

"What are you doing, then?"

"Same rules you've had since the beginning,"

"No, but Jack…"

"Jack is in his room, and this is yours,"

"Well, back at the cabin…."

"No," He interrupts me.

"This is not the cabin. This is his house, and in here, you have rules,"

CHAPTER 40

I found the cellphone under a pile of dirt. My dad was inside the kitchen when I found it, but I ran behind my window and climbed in.

So much secrecy, I couldn't even walk outside the house without feeling guilty. The phone was broken or something that when I pressed buttons, nothing was happening. I have to get this thing fixed. There is no way around it, I must.

One night, I even tried walking outside to see if it needed moonlight. How the hell was I supposed to know how it worked? But as I walked back inside, my mom stood by the dining table, and I froze. I hid the keys behind me, the ones I got in case I was to drive out, but I am sure she heard the keys jitter. She walked to me and held me by my shoulders,

"Find her, please…." She cried.

She fell back into the chair and held her head

in her hands. I saw tears dripping off her nose. And my heart was broken. I've watched my mom suffer enough. I had to tell her something. I swung my arm forward and placed the keys on the table in front of her. She sighed and stopped crying immediately. She looked up with a mortified look on her face.

"What are you doing?" She asked. "I'm trying to find Carol, mom," I said. She grabbed the keys and placed them inside the drawer. "No, not tonight,"

"I will go tomorrow morning,"

"Yes, please…"

She walked away but I sat there for an hour. Before, I wanted to find Carol just for the pleasure of knowing she made it. But now, it was for my mom. I needed to find someone who knew how to fix cellphones.

"Where are you going?" Dad asked in the morning. "I told you, honey," Mom said. "She wants to stop by and grab a schedule of upcoming classes at the adult center,"

"You want to go back to school? For what?"

"Distraction, Andrew. God knows we all need it," Mom looked at me and nodded. It was my signal to go, and I did. And as I drove out, my dad stood by the door with an angry look on his face. He knew we were lying. But that didn't matter right now, I had to get that cellphone working again.

CHAPTER 41

The house has been quiet all week. Same room. Same food. Same times.

This isn't right!

I've been here long enough. Did I piss him off? Did he die? I don't even know if he's alive.

It feels like I've been sucked into a vortex big enough to make me feel like I'm floating in a time standing space. What the hell! Ugh!

I turn around and pull the iPod from the drawer. Dead. Oh, come on!

Jack needs to help me with this thing. I open the door and see Jay walking up the stairs.

"Jay, what's going on?"

"With what?"

"With Jack, how's Jack?"

"He's ok,"

"Are you sure?"

"Yes, just resting,"

"Why am I still here?"

"Where did you want to be?"

"I don't know, but this isn't right,"

"Kate, this is it. We do nothing else,"

"No, but"

"*But* I suggest you drop it,"

"Where's Eric?"

"He's busy,"

"Fine, then I want to go. Jack said I could go when he got better,"

"That's a lie,"

"Why do you say that?"

"Because he's the one that said to keep you in here,"

I walk past him and through the double doors as Jay rushes behind me. He grabs my arm and pulls me.

"Kate, you're back in the house. Things don't change here,"

"That's bullshit,"

"Just go back to your room,"

"Look, Jay, you either let me, or I will force myself in,"

"Kate…"

"Come on, Jay. I don't think Jack will mind me being here,"

"I do mind," Jack says behind me.

I turn to see Jack standing by his door. Then, he walks and sits on his bed. He acts like no one is here. He lays back, drinks and turns on his cigarette.

And I turn to Jay, who also stares at him.

"Jack," I say.

"I'm in no mood to deal with you right now,"

He leans back, lifts his feet, and continues watching TV.

"I just wanted to ask how you were. I can't do that?" I say as Jay tugs on my arm. Jack glances over, and Jay pulls me into the hallway. He closes the door and grabs me by my shoulders.

"Kate, we don't need this right now." He says as he pulls me towards my room. I push him away and swing Jack's door open. "Jack…"

"No, go away," he interrupts me.

Jay pulls me and I slam the door closed. He grabs my hand and I swing it away.

"Stop!" I shout. "I got it…" I say as I walk to the room. Jay walks in behind me and notices. "Jack gets in a bad mood when shit doesn't go right, Kate," he mumbles. "He just needs to get back on track. He's not ok because he's focused mostly on you,"

"What?"

"He usually isn't that careless. They've been getting closer every time. Because of you...."

"Me?"

"Look, I might be wrong. But I know you take his focus away,"

"Why?"

"Because you look like *her*...." Jay pauses but I don't want him to.

What the hell does he mean?

"What the hell are you talking about?"

His face becomes serious, and he shakes his head. He rapidly picks up the trash bag and I run to the door and slam it shut, leaving him inside.

"What are you talking about?" He pushes me aside, but he is not getting away. "Jay..." I say, but he forces himself out.

Oh no.

That's why I am here.

That's why he treats me like that, because of her.

I look like her.

I look like Lisa.

CHAPTER 42

Looking for Carol was nerve-wracking. I drove to the convenience store at the corner and stared out the window for a while. Not a single person walked in within twenty minutes of being there. That they still had their doors open to the public was unbelievable to me.

A woman stepped out. She threw a trash bag and walked back inside. I parked my car across the street and walked in. "Hi," I said and the man nodded.

I placed the cellphone on the counter, and he stared at me, puzzled. "What do you need?" He crossed his arm. I looked up at the clock, knowing he was trying to rush me. "I don't know. This doesn't work. I've tried playing with it. I tried pushing the buttons, but…" He flipped the cellphone open and stared at it for a few seconds. He shut it back down and slid it towards me. "No battery," he said.

"Batteries? Like, which ones?" I asked. He smiled, amused at my inexperience. "No, you don't get them. You need to charge the phone using a cord." He said. "What is that? How do I do that?" I asked.

"We don't carry any, but we know of a store in Sacramento that has them," He leaned down, picked up a piece of paper, and wrote an address down. He handed me the paper, and I read it.

Sacramento.

I knew it.

"They will be able to help me?"

"That is a cellphone store. If there is any place that knows about cellphones, it's that one," I started walking out as he mumbled something else.

"Excuse me?"

"But I would wait. They don't open early. I think they open at 2 PM," he said.

I sat in my car for hours. Staring at the convenience store as one person came in and out every few minutes now. I was sweating when it wasn't even hot.

Contemplating my drive, I stared at the dusted cellphone in my hand. I had to make the drive; there was no way around it. It was the only way I could find Carol, and I was not going to let this cellphone issue get in the way.

I promised my mom.

I needed to find Carol for her.

If I just knew she was ok and on her way to Europe, then everything would go back to normal, and the feeling of not knowing wouldn't be eating us alive.

I rested my head on the window and shut my eyes, drifting off to sleep, unknowingly, in the middle of a broken city.

CHAPTER 43

I stand at the top of the stairs and stare into the basement. If no one is going to help me, then I will help myself. I come to the basement looking for Eric. He always knows what to say.

The door is cracked open, but there is no one inside. I look to the kitchen, and my stomach growls. My curiosity growls stronger. I go downstairs and stand before the machine. I know I shouldn't be here, but I know what this thing can do.

It is shockingly intimidating, though. I feel a little weak in the knees, but I sit in front of it, nonetheless. A metal chain-link cage surrounds the computer. Jack must have installed it since he thought someone was down here.

Right now, it is open, though.

There is a bright blue square at the right upper corner of the screen, and it's blinking. *SEARCH*.

What the hell is the search?

Oh. Yeah.

That is where Eric entered information the last time I was here. I turn back and stare at the box blinking, calling me to enter something into it. I slowly run my fingers through the keyboard, and I am tempted.

Oh, come on! Just do it!

I type the letter C, followed by the A, and so on.

Finally, typing Carol's full name. *Carol Preston.*

The screen turns red, and I stare down at the keyboard. A red button glows, and I press it. The machine turns black, and the rest of the screens turn on. Loud noises start to beep, and I stumble backward.

DELETE! DELETE!

The device goes crazy, and the screens turn green. "Oh my God! They're gonna kill me!" I scream. I run upstairs, swing the door open, but I am stopped by Jack coming downstairs.

Fuck!

He freezes as he sees me come out of the basement and then investigates the basement, assuming Eric is down here with me. He looks into the kitchen and then turns to me. He didn't even need to talk, I knew what he needed from me.

An answer. "Uh…" I can't bring myself to say

anything before he moves me to the side and walks down the basement to see what I did. I take a step back, hoping to walk upstairs without repercussion but he calls me over.

And as I walk downstairs, he types something on the keyboard, and the original screen comes on, back to normal. He brings up another screen, and what I entered is shown across all screens.

He looks back at me and then back at the screens again.

"You, you're not mad?"

He runs his hand over his head,

"I'm furious," he smiles. "What were you doing?" I grab a chair and sit next to him, and he looks over. "What were you doing?" He brings up Carol's name.

"Carol Preston?"

"My sister,"

He looks back at the screen and keeps entering information. Looks like babble to me. He types away and places an earpiece in his ear. He connects a box to a large screen, and he remains there for a couple of minutes. After a few minutes, the machine beeps, and we see a list of girls that have the same name as Carol.

"Boulder Creek Circle, there she is!" I shout.

Then, Jack starts working on it some more. He

clicks away at some things, and he moves boxes around; he disconnects others.

And I am here.

Happy.

Jack sighs and puts his head down.

"If I find something, something bad, do you want me to tell you?" I stay silent, and he lifts his eyebrows, waiting for my response.

"Of course…" I reply.

He presses a red button, and a word comes up on the screen: *VOICE RECOGNITION*.

He connects a wire to the black box, and there is static. He moves another button on the black box and pulls the wire out of his ear, handing it to me.

"You're not gonna like it," he says as he gives me the earpiece, and my heart drops. I can feel the sweat on my hands as I grab the earpiece and hold it near my ear.

"Kate, answer me. It's Carol, can you hear me? Kate! Oh God, help me. Please…"

I stare blankly at the screen as I hear Carol's insistent voice coil up inside of my throat. Jack looks at me and pulls my chair towards him. The sound of her begs hit me like a boulder against a weakened bone.

Everything I feared is true.

She didn't make it.

She needs help. Jack places his hand on my thigh.

"Hey," He whispers as I wipe my eyes.

She needs help, and she called me for it! I wasn't there for her! Jack wipes my tears with his shirt, and I lower my head away from him.

"Find out more, please!"

"I can't...."

"Why?"

"This thing tracks anything she might have used,"

"And?"

"Kate, this voicemail is dated back to April. It's September. This means three things:"

"What?"

"That she either made it out to Europe, and I can't track her. She is somewhere unsafe, or"

"Or what?"

"Or she's dead."

CHAPTER 44

"Please, find out more!"

Jack leans back on his chair and covers his face.

"You have to find out more. You have to!"

"Kate," He shakes his head.

No. That's wrong. She isn't dead. She isn't. He can find out more. I stumble and slam my shoulder on the gate. I drop to my knees on the stairs.

Breathing a little harder. I can't accept that. She was a tough girl, and I was sure she is ok. She always knew how to get away with things.

Jack walks behind me and pulls me up. My knees are about to give up, and Jack places his hand on my back.

"You have to find out more,"

"I just showed you everything I found,"

I stand and grab the keyboard off the table. I

hand it to him, and he holds it with a puzzled look on his face.

"I told you, that's all I can do,"

"Tell me you are lying,"

"I'm not...."

"You mean to tell me that you can't find out where someone is?"

"I did find her,"

I stare at the screen flashing before me, and I am in disbelief. This can't be it. No. I won't accept that.

"Look, I know you're upset," he says as I walk past him and push him out of the way. He stumbles and falls onto the chair.

"Watch it," he says as he holds his chest. He leans into his legs and watches me. And I can't stay put. I walk around the cage, thinking of ways to search for her. Maybe she went to Sacramento and then found a way to San Francisco. He has to look in San Francisco. She must be missing because she is on a plane to Europe.

She was. She made it out.

Jack stands and walks to the door.

"Let's go," he says.

"This is all your fault,"

"My fault? How the fuck?" he laughs.

I stare at the screen and cover my face with my palm. My head is heavy, my body is hot, and I am angry. I try biting my lip, holding my tongue, but I can't.

"It's not my fault she snooped with these fucking people,"

"I don't know, Jack. You guys are all alike,"

"What the fuck," he laughs.

"You guys do this. You rip girls from their homes: kidnapping, raping and without…" Jack laughs out loud. He shakes his head from side to side.

"This is what I'm getting for finding out where your sister is?" He says.

"You didn't find her,"

"Now I understand why she got herself in trouble…."

"What does that mean?"

"If she has the same fucking attitude as you do, they would have killed you too," I stare at him. Annoyed.

"Well, you want me here. Deal with it," I mumble. He laughs again and throws himself in the chair. He grabs a liquor bottle from behind the screen and smiles as he lifts it in a cheering way.

"Fuck, Kate, you really live in your little world, don't you?" He unscrews the cap and pours some into the lid. He is about to sip it when I smack his hand and it drops. He stares at me without moving a muscle. He shakes his head, and I stand in front of him. Waiting for another moment so I can smack him on the face instead.

"Watch it with that attitude,"

"You care about me. I know you won't hurt me,"

"I care about you?"

"You do. That's why you've protected me from everything that's happened,"

"I just don't want to clean blood stains off my truck," he says as he drinks directly from the bottle instead.

"You're lying,"

"Sorry, beautiful, I don't mess with hostages."

SMACK! A slap across the face, and I stand still. My hand balls into a fist, and I am waiting. Fucking do something! Ugh! I hate his dumbass! I want to get him angry. I want to get back at him. My insides are scalding, and my hands shaky. I can feel my jaw clenching enough to break my teeth. "No wonder Lisa left you!" I shout as Jack launches himself towards me right as soon as I finished saying it. I shriek as he pulls me by the back of my neck and slams me into the chair. "Let me go!" I shout.

"Don't you dare bring her up!"

"Let me go! Ouch! You are fucking hurting me! Don't touch me!"

He kicks the chair I am sitting on, and there I go, slamming into the floor. "No! Shouting doesn't work with you! I've tried being nice!" he shouts.

"Fine!" I scream.

He turns away and swings the entire cage closed.

Oh no!

"What are you doing?! JACK!" I scream as I slam my body into it. He is going to lock me in! Dear God, no!

"Jack!" I scream again, and he places his body against the door. He starts mumbling words, and I am pushing with everything I have.

"Jack! I'm afraid, please, I hate the dark!"

"It doesn't work. You never listen!"

"I'll listen! I swear!"

"No, you need to learn well!"

"I will, please, let me out!"

"No!"

"Jack, please!"

"You wanted to be a bird? There!"

"No, Jack!"

"There's your little fucking birdcage!"

CHAPTER 45

A car went by, and I realized I was still in front of the convenience store. There were sweat stains on my shirt, and the heatwave was spewing out of the concrete road.

2 PM! Shit! I fell asleep for five hours!

I drove to Sacramento, and I noticed I was driving at ninety miles per hour, but that didn't matter. I couldn't waste any more time.

Entering Sacramento was like entering a pathway towards hell. It was humid, dirty, and smelled rancid. Sacramento was yet another dust bowl. The billboards that were once giant televisions were now broken and faded. Tagged graffiti covered the concrete walls and sides of the freeway.

It was heartbreaking. But I look at the paper.

Florin Road.

Driving into the city was even more shocking than going through the freeway. People sleeping in cardboard boxes, one after another, lined up along the sidewalk. Some of them stood up as they saw me driving. I drove faster, noticing that more of them would gather up and stare.

I pulled into the shop. A shabby little shop near a broken-down gas station. Surely, this wasn't the correct address. The windows were covered in plywood. I thought the store was closed for a moment, but then I saw a sign sprayed on the side that said it was open.

Walking inside was a mistake.

Several cellphones hung on the wall, and gadgets were across the tables. Across the room were swords on display and a couple of handguns were over a counter to my side. After noticing the guns, I stepped back and reached for the door, but a short man came out from the back.

"How can I help you?" I stared at him, but I remained at a distance. "I'm a businessman, not a crook. Don't you worry," he said with a heavy accent. I walked up to him and pulled out the cellphone. I slid it across the counter. He picked it up and stared at me,

"Do you know what this is?" He asked, waving the cellphone in my face. "A cellphone," I said. He laughed, and I laughed too, trying to cover up how stupid I might have sounded.

"A couple of years ago, Vexnet created a phone that was also a tracking device. This wasn't like Track my Phone bullshit. This was better. No internet was needed. But, of course, yes. This one was only a prototype, though. Never really made the market. Tell me, how did you get a hold of it?" He said.

"It doesn't work. I need it to work," I said as he took the phone, flipped it, and turned it on. " I may have broken it. Can you fix it?" I asked.

"You don't know much about these things, do you?" He asked as I shook my head.

"It was my sisters…."

He walked to the back and brought out a couple of cords, "I'm telling you; this was a prototype. These things didn't have a charger, but I can find one, hold on," he said as he pulled several cords from a drawer. He plugged one and nothing. He plugged another and nothing. He must have plugged in about five different ones when one finally worked. And a soon as he plugged in the last one, the phone beeped.

He lifted his head, unplugged it, and tossed it on the table. "Get out of here, you! Get out!" He shouted. I stood back and lifted my hands in front of him.

"What? Please help me, please… I don't know what it's doing," I said.

"I'm telling you, get out of my store! Get out of here with that thing!"

I grabbed the cellphone and stuck it in my purse, "At least let me buy that thing," I asked, pointing at it. He walked back, went to the side, and unplugged the cable.

"$87.50. Hurry, get out of my store!" He said.

"If you don't know what this is, then be careful with this thing," he said right before I exited.

"I won't need it long," I replied.

"It doesn't matter. Make sure you turn it off once you use it,"

I thanked him and stepped out.

CHAPTER 46

"Jack!" I scream.

I pull but this thing is bolted down. I slam my hands and press my body against it. I turn around and looked around. The smell of musk is causing me sickness. The darkened crevices under the tables and the holes on the concrete wall are freaking me out.

"Jack!" I cry.

I slam my body backward and drop onto the floor. "Please…" I sigh, trying to breathe. I was sinking. I was falling into an abyss, and I was abandoned once again.

He isn't going to come back!

I am the devil's plaything and he could care less!

Maybe he will come in a few minutes.

But he didn't. It's been hours since Jack left, and

I am still sitting here by the doorway. My butt aches, my leg is cramped, and I have nothing left in me.

My head feels like a balloon.

What's that sound?!

A few clicks followed by a hiss. I sit up and move away. I swear this thing can cut my skin by the amount of pressure I was giving it. A tingling sensation all over my legs, and I slam down. Weak.

I stare at the corner where the sounds are coming from, and I see a furnace.

Oh, my God!

My head falls into my knees.

Crying.

I can't even say I am hungry because no one knows I'm here. And Jack will not help me at all. I try to sleep it through, but the rattling pipes keep me up. And right at 2 AM, the entire basement goes dark. No light out the window, no sounds upstairs; complete and utter silence.

I don't like this.

I don't…

"Jack!!" I scream again as my body stiffens. I want to leave! I want to go home! I hold onto my stomach, and I am in tears. I lay on my back and stare at the ceiling. A blue light flickers and I am holding onto the tiniest light as a fragment of hope.

I woke up and lurched up. I don't even know what time it is anymore.

Is it sunrise? Sunset?

The color of the sky is somewhat confusing, and I am not sure if I slept through or haven't slept at all—my stomach grumbles.

I am hungry.

I lay back down and place my head against the cage, holding myself in contempt. You went too far, idiot. The amount of time I've been struggling is not fair. I have done not a single damn thing to these people. It would be better if he just went ahead and shot me.

That's it. Bye-bye.

The morning shines through the window. I rub my eyes and notice a plate of food on the floor next to me. Like a fucking dog. I shove the pieces of food in my mouth right away. I crank open the water bottle and gulp down at least half of it.

Oh, sweet mercy! I can feel every crevice of my mouth suddenly quenched.

But my stomach hurts, and I lay down. I feel humiliated. How sad! How stupid! I close my eyes, hoping to make this all go away, but it doesn't. I am here, again. I could have left, but I decided to stay.

I did. For this?

The door opens. I stand up and go beside the door. Jack's muffled voice is outside. He opens the door and walks downstairs.

Then, he stands before the cage and smiles.

Idiot.

He grabs his keys and unlocks it. He swings it open and stands there, looking at me from top to bottom. I think he notices my dirty clothes and messed-up hair. I feel my hands shaking.

Calm down. But I fail.

I swing the bottled water at him, and it slams into his chest but he doesn't react. He shakes his head, locks the cage again, and stands there. I turn around and he sighs a heavy sigh but doesn't say anything. The room becomes dark again, and I see him walking upstairs without saying a word.

A few hours pass by, and I see the nightfall again.

The little bit of food I ate helps me get better. I recover a little bit of strength. My stomach feels better, and the nausea is gone. And for the moment, I forget about Jack. I forget where I am and what is happening to me. My world becomes another, and I am thinking of Carol now.

I think of Carol and Europe.

Why were Aunt Megan and Carol so excited about Europe?

I never understood.

What does Europe have that is so amazing?

And Carol…

Is she there? Did she make it?

What would she be doing?

She loved shopping. She loved wearing big hats and dresses. I picture her living in the 50s with the type of dresses she wore. She had one particular red dress and with her red hair, it was one of my favorite wardrobes.

Something I can never pull off. I couldn't be her. She was far too brave and beautiful.

I miss her; I miss Carol.

I sit in front of the computer, and I notice the box attached to the screens. The search button blinks.

It calls me.

The one where he entered Carol's name.

I see a button that says, "History," and I click it and it punches my stomach. Carol's pictures come up. Carol at a party. Carol's school ID picture. Carol with friends, Carol. Carol. Carol. And I am in tears.

A hollow feeling creeps inside me, and I failed

her. We had many arguments about the house, arguments about her partying. Never once did I understand what freedom meant to her. She was caged up inside our home, just as I am here. And I know what she felt at home, now.

I press a button, and her voice embraces me again.

"Kate, answer me. It's Carol, can you hear me? Kate! I need your help. Oh God, help me. Please…"

Her words recoil inside my stomach, and I feel debilitated. The worst part was that I couldn't do anything to help her anymore. I thought she was strong enough to get out of trouble and I am hopeful that she made it out, hopeful that she did get away with Derek, whether Sacramento or San Francisco.

Carol is a trooper. She always has been. I stare at the pictures on the computer with blurry eyes. She made it; I know she did. I'm just disappointed because I never got to tell her how much I will miss her. I closed my eyes and began pressing the same button over and over, just to hear her voice.

"Kate, answer me. It's Carol, can you hear me? Kate! I need your help. Oh God, help me. Please…"

"I'm sorry, Carol. I was never a good sister; I always made you feel like crap when you were trying to make me feel alive,"

"Kate, answer me. It's Carol, can you hear me? Kate! I need your help. Oh God, help me. Please..."

"I hope you're ok. I hope you're in a better place than me."

"Kate, answer me. It's Carol, can you hear me? Kate! I need your help. Oh God, help me. Please..."

"I envy you, sister. I envy your courage, your gut. Your will to live. I hope to have that someday if I ever get out of here. If I never get to see you again, just know that I love you so much. Now I know you are that bird Aunt Megan was talking about."

CHAPTER 47

Maybe this thing will help me understand what everyone is talking about. I erase her name from the search bar and enter Europe instead. The thing that Carol and Aunt Megan wanted all their lives. The place that makes everything better.

And suddenly, I fall back into my chair, and my eyes do not blink for a moment. Europe.

Wow. Takes a breath out of me.

There are buildings built like castles, brick walls all around, and beautiful green pasture around an entire city. A river surrounds another; rustic boats carry people through them and there are cities with arches and medieval structures, and oh, my God, they are impressive!

I come across an image that left me speechless.

A city with glowing lights with a gigantic triangular structure built directly in the middle of it all.

I click on the image, and another one comes up. Pictures from different locations; images taken from boats, hotel rooms, castles, and houses can all see the structure. A red, blue, and white flag flies across the rock-paved city.

"The tour eiffel," I read.

That. That right there. That is my Europe. I stare at the lights shining down into the city. I stared at the smiling faces of people gathered underneath. I stare at the colors of the sky; I can't believe there is something so beautiful out there. There is my dream. There is where I want to go.

I found it.

I now understand what Aunt Megan and Carol were excited about. I finally found my dream. I want to be at the "Tour Eiffel."

And after a few seconds, melancholy hits.

These cities, surrounded by such beauty, are so far away from me—instant regret. I feel stupid for not taking the opportunity to leave when Eric offered. I lay back on the chair and leave the image of the Tour Eiffel on one screen and Carol's photograph on another.

"Your sister is pretty," Jack says as he walks down the stairs. I turn around and slide my chair to the corner, pushing the keyboard to the side. He walks down, removes the lock, and opens the gate. He walks up to the computer and pulls a chair to sit down in front of it.

He looks at me and then stares back at the screen.

"Paris? Really?" He asks.

"What's Paris?"

"That picture. The city is called Paris,"

"Oh,"

"France is a long way from here, you know?"

I remain silent, sitting by the corner of the cage and I stare at the open gate and keep staring back at Jack. After a few minutes, he shuts off the computer.

"Do you want to go back up?"

"I don't care,"

"Either you go with me, or you'll stay here another two days,"

"You kept me here that long?"

"Did you learn your lesson?"

I remain quiet. He left me here to starve, dry rot stuck inside this basement?

"To be honest, you reek. You need a shower,"

My mouth trembles and he notices. How could he do that? How could someone treat another like a dog? Jack sighs, lowers his head, and runs his hand through his face.

"You're right. I'll stop. Let's go."

And as we walk upstairs, and I enter the living room, I drop. The light is far too bright, and I am disoriented in an instant. I fall back into the wall, and I shut my eyes. Jack rushes to pick me up and covers my eyes,

"Shut your eyes," he says as he grabs me by my shoulders. I move forward, and my knee gives out. I slam onto the ground, and I shriek as I hear my knee pop as I slam into the floor.

"What the fuck, Jack? You said she was ok down there!" Eric shouts.

"She is just disoriented,"

"This is fucked up! I told you about that!"

"I know,"

"Let me take her. You're going to kill her!"

"I'm gonna help her!"

Eric leans in to grab my arm but Jack tosses Eric's hands out of the way. Eric forces himself to me as Jack grabs him by his jacket, pulls him, and tosses him up into the wall and keeps him there.

"Don't you fucking touch her!"

"We don't do this, Jack! Get your fucking head straight! Stop taking your anger out on her!" Jack lets him go, and just as Jack bends down to pick me up,

Eric says something. Something that makes Jack furious in an instant.

"Kate is not Lisa, Jack…." He mumbles.

Jack freezes as I look up. He shuts his eyes and swings his fist right onto Eric's face. Eric stumbles, and falls. Then, he launches forward and strikes back at Jack. I shriek as Jay comes in, running from another room. He grabs Jack and swings him out of Eric, and Eric stumbles upward.

"Be pissed at me for whatever reason, man, but you know I'm fucking right!" he shouts as Jack dusts himself and pushes Jay out of the way. Jay holds him, as Eric storms out of the room yelling something.

Jack stays quiet but comes for me and helps me walk to my room. And when we go in, he asks me about my knee.

"I'm sorry, Kate." He says. "For everything,"

I don't know what to say so I stay quiet.

"Take a shower. I will leave you alone. I promise."

CHAPTER 48

What the hell just happened? Why am I still here? That fight with Eric and Jack told me what I needed to hear. I have to go. They will only get worse. I don't want to be here anymore.

Please, I don't want to near them.

As I step into the bathroom, I catch a glimpse of myself, and I realize. Paris is never going to happen. I don't even have a car or a home to go to. What makes me think Paris is even an option? I am stuck here.

And I chose this, too. I blew my chances of ever getting out. If Jack doesn't get to murder me, I am sure they will do it somehow.

And then I look at myself in the mirror once again. And I smile. Who is that person? This person who stands before me? Why does she have dreams?

I see someone new, and I don't know if I like her. She wants to be free. She feels emotions. Sometimes, those emotions aren't the best ones, but she has them, nonetheless.

And even when I am where I am, I feel ok. I don't feel like a robot anymore. I smile because I know that someday, I'll be free. When the day comes, I know the Tour Eiffel will still be there, whether I visit in a human form or another.

My clothes fall on the floor, and I slowly step into the bathtub. I sit in hot water and I swimmer in it. I lay my head back and stare at the steam coming off my body. Humidity has now surrounded the bathroom air, and I breathe in every stress, pain and agony felt inside. I breathe out, lean my body downwards and put my head back.

Soothing as it is, the sound of the water running is very relaxing. I let my ears fall underwater, and I hear the stream from underneath. I lay back, and the water rises to my face. I close my eyes and imagine the beauty of Europe and the beauty it would be if I could be there.

My head sinks.

I take a deep breath and allow the water to cover my face completely. Something is comforting about this. Without breathing, I am at peace. The red tint of my eyelids becomes black. And a euphonious feeling embraces me. I feel like I am dying, sinking into a hole of emotions, and I am ok with that. I am ok.

A pull startles me, and I gasp for air as Jack pulls me out of the bathtub with brute force.

"What the fuck are you doing!?" he shouts.

He turns my body around and smacks my back a couple of times. He lifts me and drops me into the bed, holding my neck with his hand.

"Kate!" he shouts, but his voice is muffled. He panics, presses my stomach, and turns me around. My body is crawling with goosebumps, and I place my hand on Jack's face, but he smacks it away,

"This is not fucking funny!" He shouts.

The room is blurry, and Jack grabs my face as he shouts towards the door. The room becomes obscure. He lifts me and rushes to his room. Eric comes over and gives Jack a bag. Jack frantically searches through it, and Eric hovers over me with a nervous look on his face.

Jay rushes in as Jack closes my nose. He blows air into my mouth, and I feel pressure on my throat. A bunch of water comes running out of my mouth, and I lean sideways to throw up. I hear them breathing heavily. A sigh of relief, and they wait for me to do anything else.

Jack lifts my hair and checks my face. I was drowning, and I didn't even know.

"Jack, she'll die next time," Eric mumbles.

Jack keeps me held up against him. He places his arm around my head and breathes. His heart beats fast.

"You're going to kill her," Jay adds.

"I know…"

"She should go away," Eric says.

"I know."

"Think about that,"

They grab the bag and leave and Jack whispers something, but I don't understand. He lays me back down and lays my head down slowly on the pillow. I want to talk. I want to say something, but I have no strength left in me. My throat hurts.

All I have is pain. Again.

I drift to sleep, and the room goes silent. I open my eyes a few hours later and notice the night outside the window. I lift myself with my elbow and see Jack smoking next to me.

"What the hell were you doing?" He asks.

He turns the cigarette off a little aggressively.

"Nothing,"

"You were submerged completely underwater!"

"I was just taking a bath. I didn't know."

He sits at the edge of the bed and covers his face.

He then rests his arms on his thighs and stares blankly towards the window.

"Jack" I say as I grab his arm.

"What…"

"I didn't even know I was doing that,"

"I don't do this, Kate. I don't hurt people that way. I'm not like that. I don't mean to hurt you. I'm sorry I keep fucking up,"

"I know,"

"I just don't know what to do. I'm an idiot. I've hurt you. I don't want to, but I do. Without even knowing I'm doing it. I see myself fucking up, Kate, and I hate myself for it. It freaks me out to think it's because…" He stops himself and chokes a little bit.

A pause longer than expected. He pats his chest and holds it.

"Because what?"

"Because you look like her."

I know Jay said that exact thing but hearing it from Jack was even more awful. "I hate to think that's the reason. Because I fucking hate her,"

"If you hate her so much then why am I here?" He smiles. "Because when I first saw you, I wanted to make you suffer because of her."

I shift uncomfortably, and he shakes his head.

"But as time went by, I found that I don't want to hurt you. You're a different person. You're caring, and you have a good heart." He wipes his forehead and sighs. "Shit. I've tried. I failed many times, but I know I fucking tried."

"So, why am I here?"

"Because I like having you with me. There's something about you that makes sense to me. When you're near, I don't feel insane anymore and I'm fucking selfish."

He grabs his drink. "Plus, where are you going to go? I fucked up, and now, you have nowhere to go," Jack holds his head, and his hair falls onto his face.

I get close to him and pull his hair back over his head. "Do you want to leave?" He asks. "I know you want to." I do, and I don't. But I can't bring myself to say it.

"You had the chance to leave twice. Why didn't you?"

"I don't know. I guess you make sense to me, too."

CHAPTER 49

Jack lifts and walks into the bathroom, and I hear him grunt. I know it's the pills again. I grab the trash can and start dumping the pills left beside the nightstand. He swings the door open and asks me what I am doing. He leans against the drawer and watches me as I throw away pills lying around, and empty bottles of liquor tossed on the sofa.

"What are you doing?"

"You need to get better. This is not helping you."

He lifts his eyebrows and points at the trash can. "That's what that is," I shake my head, and Jack walks over to the bed. He sits at the edge of it and looks at me.

"That takes the pain away, you know."

"By the look you give me, you know that's not right,"

He stares at me as I open the drawer next to the window, where I had seen the bag of pills before. I grab the bag and toss it in the trash.

"You don't want to get better," and he doesn't do anything. He looks at me. I walk over and stand before him. He gives me his hand, and I hold it. Then, I kneel before him. My finger runs through his eyebrows and down to the dark circles below his eyes.

"You don't want to get better," I whisper.

He pulls away from my hands and laughs.

"You're so dramatic,"

"All that energy you say you're putting into not hurting me, maybe you should put some of that aside for you,"

He stays quiet and turns his face away, but I grab it. He looks at me and doesn't move. He closes his eyes, and I grab his face with both my hands.

He sighs.

I touch his eyebrows and run my finger down to his nose and slowly across his lips. And as my finger drags across his lips, he opens his eyes and stares into mine without moving them. No anger anymore.

Just composure.

He focuses on me, just as I am on him, and for a moment, he smiles so subtly. I pull his face and press my lips against his. And he doesn't pull away. I rest my hands behind his neck, and he lets me kiss him.

My lips move down to his neck, and he breathes in a little deeper. He grabs my face and pulls me. He holds a lock of my hair and places it behind my ear as his hands circle my face and then down to my waist. Then, he lifts, and his kisses become more intense.

A little more force, a little more hunger.

Like he's been wanting me for a long time, even before the cabin.

My face is hot, and the more he runs his hands down my body, the hotter I get. His shirt comes off, and he lays me on my back, against his bed and as he leans into me, he pulls my shirt up. He presses his face against my chest and over my breasts as I remove my bra and he grabs my hands and places them above me.

I pull at his belt and unbuckle it. The belt goes off and I unzip his jeans. He grabs my waist and pulls me in. He pushes my legs open with his, and he leans into me. He kisses my forehead and with one pull, he takes off my underwear.

And then, the strangest feeling.

It feels weird. Wonderful weird.

I am not sure what to do so I do what he does but he doesn't mind.

My body aches, but I want it to continue. I want to see his face. I want to bite him and do everything to him. He grabs my butt and lifts me and with one swoop, I am on top. He puts his hands behind his head and lets me take charge. I am able to see him; to appreciate everything.

I am trying to stay silent, but I can't.

My body decided by itself that I can't.

And after a moment, he forcefully throws me down into the bed again and lifts my legs over his shoulders. He grabs my neck and passionately kisses me. Desperate. Frantic. Fervently.

"Look at me," he whispers as I close my eyes.

"Kate…" He whispers.

I open my eyes, and he smiles.

I pull at the blankets, at his hair and grab onto his back—anything to keep me feeling like this. I listen to the moans, the sweat, the heavy breathing, and the bed creaking.

Everything.

My body tenses. I shake as he drops over my body. And I knew, I wanted to be here forever.

CHAPTER 50

The TV light flickers, and I notice Jack's arm around me. I look at him and he looks calm. I kiss him on the forehead, and he wakes up. He gives me a crooked smile and leans in to rest his head on top of mine.

I don't want to let him go.

And the TV again:

"The European Government increasingly denies American Refugee passports. The agency will stop receiving new applications in November of this year. This leaves Americans without options. Anyone coming from America will be investigated, and a full background check will be performed before any residential permits are to be ascribed."

"I've always wanted to go to Europe," Jack says.

"Why can't you go?"

"I'm stuck,"

He puts on his boxers and walks to the bathroom. What is he stuck on? I don't understand. Moments later, he comes out.

"Can't you put someone else in charge?"

"It's not about what I do,"

I have a feeling it was because of his family.

"I just can't." he adds.

"Look. I don't know what you went through, Jack. But I know it can get better,"

He sits on the bed and looks exceptionally uncomfortable, more so than before. The TV lights up his face, and his breathing changes. I feel sadness spewing from him as he lays back down and stares.

"Lindsey and Jonathan." He says as his voice cracks and I stop breathing a little bit.

"My kids. Lindsay used to do everything with me. Even shave. She was funny and acted like me when I'm not all angry and shit," he pauses. "And Jonathan, well, a toddler still but you would have loved him," he says as he holds his chest and shuts his eyes.

"My kids…" He stops and pats his chest, and I lay my head on him, but he turns away. I grab his chin and pull it towards me, and I stare into his eyes. I wrap my arms around him and hug him tighter than I've ever have. He grabs his drink and gulps it down.

Then, he serves another. He pours a few pills into his palm and takes them.

"You are slowly killing yourself, Jack…."

"Ah, that's bullshit! Everyone does this shit! Everyone is on three different medications. How is this different?!"

"I'm not telling you anything you don't know,"

"Well, don't tell me that shit anymore!"

"Listen, I'm just,"

"Don't!" he interrupts.

"Why are you upset?"

"Don't you think I know I have an issue?"

"Jack,"

"This is bullshit! I'm tired of all of you repeating the same shit over and over!"

"Ok. I get that. But I am worried about you,"

He calms down and I grab his hand. He takes a deep breath, and I know. I know he is struggling. I stay quiet because he knows he has an issue. He battles with that every day, and every day, he fails.

"You're beautiful, Kate."

I smile.

"Seriously, your heart is beautiful, too. Why do you put up with this shit?"

"Cuz I have to," He laughs. "And I know you struggle and I think you are a good person, be it, covered in issues."

"And I'm beautiful, too," he laughs.

"Yes, that too," I add as he shakes his head.

He leans forward and I look into his eyes. He doesn't take them away. He takes my face in his hands and gives me a soft kiss.

"I love you," I whisper.

Jack puts his head down; a red blush spreads across his face and then glances up at me.

"I do too."

CHAPTER 51

Jack's belt buckle slams against the drawer, and I turn around to see what he's doing. "Sorry," he whispers. I turn around as he adjusts his pants. He leans down to kiss me and reaches over for his keys.

"I have to do something today," he says as he grabs his shirt from the sofa. I grab my clothes from the floor and start getting ready to leave.

"What are you doing?"

" I'll head back to…" He shakes his head and I pause. He sits on the bed and wraps his arms around me. "Stay here. I won't take long."

"But it's your room…."

"Yes, a super-secret fortress with top-secret weaponry," he rolls his eyes. He stands up, grabs his keys, and sticks them in his back pocket. He opens his drawer, takes a notebook, and puts papers in it.

I guess I am staying.

"Be good," He whispers and then walks out. And I have no idea what to do. I feel I am in a secret lab, like he said. There is so much in here I want to look at, but I don't. I try to stay busy by watching TV and listening to music, but I'm bored now. I take a shower and look for a brush, and next to his brush, there is an ID.

Jack's ID. His full name. Jack Dayes.

Hmm. Oh no.

My mind wanders.

Who is Jack Dayes?

If he could pull pictures of Carol, I wonder what the machine would say if I searched his name? I want to know who he is. And I know the one place where I can get this information: the basement.

I walk downstairs and look at the time and wonder if Jack's going to be back. It's been three hours since he left. I might have to rush things up a bit. I walk downstairs to the computer and see the cage open. The bottled water is still on the floor, and my food wrap is in the trash can. No one has been here since I've been here.

What if he finds out what I'm doing?

He will lock me in here for months!

Suddenly, swallowing saliva isn't as easy anymore. But I want to know who he is. I walk up, pull up a chair, and sit in front of the computer. I hit a key on the keyboard, and the entire computers light up. I thought he had shut it down.

Mmm…

Maybe someone is here after all. But, to my amazement, the picture of the Tour Eiffel is still there.

Anyway, I type Jack's name in the search bar and press enter. The computer beeps and files drop into a corner. And on it, there is a *PRIVATE* folder, but I click it anyway. A sudden dread and sense of coldness take over me. Several pictures flash before my eyes. Pictures of Jack with his children. One after another.

A boy with light brown hair curled up with Jack on a sofa. Another picture is Jack holding his boy, surrounded by people, around games, and teddy bears hung on the wall. Another picture with Jack's little girl hugging him. Jack with his little girl helping him shave. Another picture: Jack with his boy playing darts. Jack with his girl, both wearing a crown.

And I smile, but it is filled with despair.

My heart aches.

I place my hand on my throat, and my breath is shaky.

Oh, my.

His smile. His sincere smile shines through, and the brightness of his eyes twinkle. I've never met that Jack. That Jack in those pictures is happy. He has everything.

I feel guilty looking like Lisa. I can't imagine the pain he feels when he sees me. I must remind him every day that she took his kids and went away.

And it hurts.

It hurts knowing that he might never see them again. It makes me sick knowing he might never see his children grow up, go to college, and get married.

It makes me feel embarrassed to cry for Carol. Carol is in Europe, I'm sure. Having the time of her life, living the best time, and here I am, crying for a thirty-year-old woman.

And Jack and my mom lost their kids. I can't even put myself inside my mother's shoes, either. How was I to judge what she and Jack felt? How was I to understand the pain caused by losing children and having the feeling that you might never see them again?

I feel stupid for bringing up Lisa and his kids when I did. Who the hell was I to ask or even bring them up?

I had enough.

I can't keep looking at these pictures. I must stop. I grab the box to unplug it, but I accidentally press a button, and my stomach churns. My chest crunches and my body is suddenly colder than before.

There she is.

Lisa.

A picture of Lisa.

They are in the cabin by the mountains. She is hugging him, standing in front of the cabin with their kids in the background. Her long black curls fall over her side, and her brown eyes shine through.

Oh, no. The guys were right.

I look like Lisa.

"Jack loved his kids more than anything," I hear, and I freeze in place. Eric walks downstairs and sits next to me. "I remember when Lisa said she was pregnant," He shakes his head in disappointment.

"Jack was happy. The truth is, I've never seen Jack as bad and broken as he did when they lost them,"

"They lost them?"

"Kate, his kids are dead."

A darkness sinks from the inside my stomach to the back of my spine. Tears well up in my eyes, and I wipe them. Never once did I think they would be gone that way! My mouth trembles. I am trying hard not to cry, but it was useless.

"We tried locating her. We kept tracking her

down, but we failed miserably. We finally got a call from one of the guys at the house saying that she was at their private home right behind this one. We don't even know how she got through the barricades…"

"Eric, are you telling me she hurt her own kids?"

"We tried to find her. But when we did, she was already inside their house. A couple of months ago, when they broke up, she threatened to hurt everyone, even the kids. But she got to them. We were too late. We couldn't stop the fire on time,"

"His scar…"

"He tried jumping in, but the ceiling collapsed. That's why we took him to the hospital."

"Where's Lisa?"

"She begged, but Jack shot her before she got away,"

I place my hand over my mouth, staring at Jack and Lisa's picture on the screen.

"Jack hurts every time he sees you, you know?"

"I am not her, Eric…."

I couldn't believe what she did to her kids.

I feel angry.

Completely disgusted just looking at her.

"I might look like her, but I am not her!"

"We tried catching her before she did anything

stupid, but we couldn't find her," He shakes his head and glances at me.

"We kept tracking her down to Stockton, to Sacramento, and back again to Stockton during the same goddamn day. But then we found a purse with her cellphone in it at the convenience store down French Camp Road the day we picked you up,"

A purse?

Wait…

Carol's cellphone?!

CHAPTER 52

Arriving at the convenience store was the worst thing I had ever done. I sat in front of the store for five minutes. I knew my curfew time was close, but I needed to turn the cellphone on once again. I entered the store, walked to the back, and asked the guy behind the counter to help me.

He pointed to a wall socket, and I plugged in the cord. The phone turned on and beeped twice. Then, the phone beeped louder every time. The man rushed to me, screaming at me to turn it off,

"You need to leave, now! You need to go!" He shouted,

"I'm sorry! I don't know how to use this!" I said.

He took the phone from me, shut the phone down, and handed it back. Hearing them yelling was terrifying, so I took the cord off the wall and stuck it in my purse.

That was when the truck screeched outside.

That was Jack, Eric, and Jay.

I placed my purse under the counter, but I think they found it when they took me outside.

Carol had Lisa's phone?

I was the one being followed to Sacramento and back. But how?

That cellphone belonged to Derek, Carol said.

But Derek knew Jack.

And Jack was with Lisa.

So, Carol must have hung out with Lisa all along.

CHAPTER 53

"What?" My face must have given it away because he grabs my shoulders and shakes me. "What?" he shouts.

"Did they have a brown car?"

"What does that...."

"Just tell me!"

Eric looks through some pictures and comes across Lisa and that car. I cover my mouth and cry. I press my lips shut because I want to scream. I point to it in desperation. I slam my hands on the table.

"Fucking tell me!"

"Carol...."

"What are you...."

"My sister! She left in this car before she went missing!" I pointed to it, and Eric stares at the screen, baffled.

"She went with them! Where did they go?!"

"Kate…" Eric mumbles. His voice was more profound, something sinister.

"Show me a picture of your sister," He pushes the keyboard my way as I enter Carol's name. I turn around as soon as Carol's picture pops on the screen and Eric lifts from his seat. He walks backward and hits the cage. I look at him, and his face is pale. Frightened. The flush of pink on his cheeks is gone, and his eyes; they didn't blink at all.

"What happened, Eric? What's going on?"

I grab his face and pull it down towards me, wanting to squeeze the thoughts out of his head, but he shakes his head and stares intensely at the screen.

And with immediate urgency, he grabs my arm and shuts the computer down.

"You have to leave!" He pulls me upstairs, and I pull back. I swing my arm behind me, but he pulls me even harder. "What are you talking about?" I shout as I see him pick up the keys. He rustles through some papers and starts pulling me upstairs.

"Eric, you're freaking me out! What's going on?!"

He tugs me upstairs and walks through the kitchen. He kicks the door open and takes me outside to the backyard.

"Get out of here! I know you're going to be all

right. Just go!" He says as he pulls money out of his pocket and tries handing it to me.

"What are you talking about? Eric, you're scaring me!"

Eric hastily rushes over the driver's side of the truck. "What are you doing?" I shout. Eric leans on the driver's seat, pulls wires from underneath the steering wheel, and cuts them using a pocketknife.

"There is no tracker in this car," he says as he pushes me. "Eric, stop! Do you know where she is?"

"Shh!" He says, looking upstairs to the window.

"Go, Kate. Please, go!" He begs. "you said you wanted to go to Europe, right? Here," he says as he hands me the keys and tries to give me money again.

"Eric, stop! What's going on? Is Carol in Europe?!"

"Just drive to San Francisco, towards the 80, and that will lead you to the San Francisco airport!" I slam the door, and Eric runs his fingers through his hair. He is startled. He looks around, desperate.

"Eric, stop! What the hell is going on? Do you know where Carol is?"

"Yes!" Eric looks behind him and then looks back at me. His face troubled with terror. Like he witnessed a horrible massacre, and I am hysterical. He knew where Carol was! I turn to look at the house and Eric runs his hands over his hair. Not a subtle one either. He is afraid.

"That day. When Jack lost his kids, the day he shot Lisa, she wasn't alone. She had another girl in that car…."

"What?!" I scream.

Eric pushes me inside the car, "Kate, please, go!"

"Carol was the other girl!"

"Kate, go!"

"Was it my sister?!"

"Yes! Yes, it was! It was your sister! It was that damn girl in that picture!"

"Eric…" I cry, and his phone rings. He jumps and hesitates to answer it. "Kate, go away. If Jack finds out, I can't protect you." I slam the door closed and lean on it. My feet are frail. I place my hands on my knees because I can't think clearly. Everything around me feels hot like I am burning from the inside.

"Where is she, Eric?" I scream. "Where is she?!"

"Jack doesn't know it was her, so you have to go!"

"Where?"

"Fuck, Kate…"

"Where!?"

"The house behind the pool house. About a mile away that way. The same fucking house his kids died in!"

CHAPTER 54

I don't think of anything but getting to that house. I see it at a distance, and I am not that far. I keep running, hoping that when I get there, I find what happened to Carol. Jumping every rock on the ground, I push every shrub out of the way. And when I see a burnt house, I halt.

This house is crumbled to pieces. There is nothing but a burnt-out frame. Pieces of broken wood on a pile are beside it, and this house has no rooftop.

It's destroyed.

Instead of windows, there are burnt-out holes, and it smells of musk. And to the right, an abandoned car. A striped brown car with bullet holes on the side.

And my chest tightens.

Sweat pours from my forehead and into my eyes.

The tires are blown out, and the car's color is beginning to fade. I hold onto my stomach, burning, trying to breathe, but I can't. I slowly walk to the car and close my eyes. I make my way to the passenger's side, and I see the dashboard broken.

My ears are ringing, and I am standing before my worst fear. I hear a truck rumble a mile away, and I swing the door open. I stumble and fall onto my butt, screaming. "No!" I scream.

The headrest is ripped and covered in what seems like bloodstains. The seat has red stains all around the front wheel and the dashboard. "Oh my God!" I cried as I see Carol's suitcase on the back seat.

Jack screeches to a stop and jumps out. He looks at me confused, and I stand up. "What the hell are you doing?" he shouts, but I swing my fists to hit him.

"You fucking monsters!" I scream.

"Stop! What the fuck are you doing?"

"That's Carol's shit, you fucking murderers!"

"What are you talking about?"

Another truck arrives, and Eric and Jay run to us.

Eric grabs me, and Jay pushes Jack back to the truck. "Jack! Go home, man! We'll handle this!" Jay shouts, but Jack comes back, trying to come to me. "What the fuck is going on?" I drop to my knees and cover my face.

"Oh my God, Carol!"

"It was Kate's sister, Jack…." Eric says.

"What are you talking about?"

"The other person in the car. When Lisa left, she had another person with her,"

"And?"

"It was Kate's sister."

Jack stares at me, stunned. His eyes widen as he looks at the house and then the car. He shuts his eyes and looks at the floor. Eric helps me up and pats my back, but Jack begins laughing.

We both look at him, and Jay looks at us without saying a word. Jack covers his face and shakes it. He breathes heavily and grunts.

"Jack," Eric says, but Jack holds himself on the hood of the truck.

"Hey, man," Jay adds, but Jack isn't listening. He looks forward without paying attention to us. He covers his mouth and laughs again.

And I am more terrified than ever.

"Jack, are you ok?" Eric says.

Jack mumbles something and walks back and forth. Suddenly, he walks to the truck and opens the passenger's side.

"Kate…" Eric whispers as Jack shuts the door, and

we see a gun in his hand. I scream, and Eric shouts at Jack, but Jack is walking towards me. "Stop!" Jay says, trying to push him back, but he can't. I run, but Jack grabs me as Eric tries to stand between.

"She was in it! She had to be part of all that!"

"No, I wasn't!" I scream.

"Did you have the phone, Kate?" he shouts.

"What?"

"Did you have the phone when we got you? Did you have it?"

"Jack,"

"The phone we found at the store! Answer me!"

"Yes! Yes, I did, Jack! I did!"

Jack walks over as Eric pushes him back. I fall into the house and hold myself on the wall.

"Jack! My sister gave it to me! I didn't know where it came from!"

"Bullshit!"

"I swear I didn't know it belonged to someone else!"

"We were following her!" Jack shouts at Eric. "We followed her to Sacramento, then back to Stockton while the others came here! You can't tell me they weren't working together!"

"No, Jack! I didn't know!"

Jack walks to the truck and holds himself on the hood. He rests his elbows on it and stays there as Eric stands in front of me. "You know what you fucking caused me?" Jack shouts as he walks back.

"Jack, I told you. I had nothing to do with it!"

Eric stands in front of me as Jack cocks his gun and points it at Eric's face. Jay runs over and grabs him, "Jack, man! What are you doing?" He shouts.

"Get out of my fucking way, Eric," Jack says in a deep undertone voice, like something took over him.

"She didn't know," Eric tells him calmly.

"Honest, she just found out today…." Jay says as he tries to push the gun away from Eric's face. And I am staring at Jack. Through the tears, I stare at the gun waiving in front of my face. I want to explain, but I can't move.

Eric is the only thing keeping me alive right now.

"Eric, I will shoot the fuck out of you if you don't move right now," Jack swings the gun to Eric's head, and it knocks him down. I scream as I try to run away, but Jack grabs me and pulls me back. And with one pull, he shoves me against the broken wall and wraps my fingers around my neck.

"Jack, I swear. Please! I didn't know Carol was here! You have to believe me!"

"Do you know how it felt?"

"You have to believe me...."

"Having to climb inside, trying to run upstairs when the whole fucking house fell down,"

"Jack..."

"Waking up in the fucking hospital, knowing I couldn't save them!"

"Please understand. I..."

"No! All the time wasted because we were chasing you!"

"I didn't know!"

His grip is tighter, and I am not able to move my head. Eric tries to move Jack away from me but he's too strong.

"Jack. I swear! I thought it was Derek's phone!"

"Don't lie to me, Kate!"

"I'm not! Please, you know I've been trying to find her!"

Jack lowers his head and shakes it. He loosens a little bit, and sighs. "I don't believe you, Kate..." he says with a calm voice.

"You were just like her after all," he says. My body shakes and the buzzing in my ear is loud enough to cut Eric and Jay shouting in the back.

"I'm glad she died, though," his grip tightens.

I grab his arm, but he keeps pressing me against the wall.

"Stop!" I sigh.

"I'm glad she died. Both of them."

"Jack,"

"When we got here, I shot the tires and they crashed right there," He points with the gun towards the car. "Then, I shot Lisa. No hesitation," His voice shakes.

"Jack, let me go," I cry.

His eyes focus only on me, but they are dark. The soft brown gleam glowing this morning is gone. All that is left is hate. I am not the Kate he loved this morning. I am someone else to him now.

"And guess what I did after?" He snarls.

I turn my head but he forces me to look at him. "I don't know!" I say as I push him away, but his whole body is leaning on me.

A laugh. A frightful laugh.

He scratches his forehead with the gun, and he shakes his head. He looks at Eric and Jay before looking at me again.

"I ordered these two," he points at them, "to shoot whoever was inside that car," he says as I cry out, wanting to ignore what he was saying.

"Why did I do that?"

"Jack!"

"Why did I do that, Kate?"

"Let me go…."

"Answer me! Why did I do that?"

"I don't know!"

"Because everyone involved deserves to die!"

He arms the gun and swings it to my face as I scream. The cold metal pressed against my forehead makes me panic, and I scream at Eric for help.

"Jack, stop!" they shout and Eric and Jay are struggling with Jack, but his hand is cemented on my face. I am moments away from losing everything.

And he was right; he was never going to let me go.

"Stop!" Eric shouts.

"She should pay for everything she did!"

"Jack, you don't want to do that!"

"Bullshit! She knew! All of it!"

"Jack!"

"Let me go! I will shoot all of you! Stop touching me!"

Jack's hand is cutting my breathing. The gun is burning me, the metal is hot, the sun is blazing down, and I knew he would shoot me at any moment.

I keep my eyes shut as I start crying, thinking, and waiting. I am going to die. This is it. I had many moments where I thought I was going to, but this is closer than the rest.

And then, I think of Carol and where we ended up. How fast our lives went. Aunt Megan, Carol, and I wanted freedom, and in some way, we received our unique form of freedom. I knew, at some point, that I would see Carol again.

Never once did I think it would be this way. It's funny how life works; it gives you what you wanted in a very different way. We weren't lucky enough to be born somewhere else, I guess.

Either way, I must make peace with that.

"Jack," I whisper.

I open my eyes and look straight into his eyes. Looking at the sweat pouring down his forehead, looking at the man I fell in love with and knowing how it ended.

He hates me. He wants me dead.

I stare at his perfectly shaped nose and his eyes. This isn't the man I was with this morning. Or maybe the man whom I was with doesn't exist.

I was lucky to meet someone who loved and cared for me, but I am rather unlucky that this is the same person who caused me so much pain. But even then, in this moment, it didn't matter if he had a gun pointed at my face. I knew it wasn't his fault, nor mine.

I make peace with that.

Life has other plans. Even when we fought through, life decided that it wants to rip us apart. When I came into his life, he was already entering a nightmare. It didn't matter how many times we tried; the shackles of misery kept pulling us apart. There was no fixing this.

There is no way he will ever hold, kiss, and tell me he loves me anymore.

And all I want to do is to tell him one last time.

Maybe just before he pulls the trigger.

"Jack…" I cry. "I love you.…"

CHAPTER 55

A gunshot.

Loud enough to cover the sound of my screams.

I drop to the floor, paralyzed. The sun blinds me, and for a moment, I look at Jack standing before me, holding himself on the wall. I quickly crawl to the side, and Eric helps me up. I turn to Jack and see the gun dropped on the floor. A bullet hole on the side of the wall away from me, not even close.

He doesn't move. He doesn't say anything. He is breathing hard, and I am staring. Eric looks through my body, but quickly realizes that Jack didn't shoot me.

Jack shot the wall instead.

Jack grabs his hair and pulls it behind his head. I wipe my eyes, clearing the tears off my face, and Jack dusts his pants. He sharply turns and walks to the truck. "Get her out of my face," he says as he walks past us, but he doesn't look at me anymore.

And just like that, he drives away.

I drop to my knees and scream into a cry. I can't breathe. Eric grabs my arm, and I swing it away, "Let me go!" he stands back. Everything came out of me, anger, sadness, desolation, fear. Everything turned into a scream, into my cries and Jay kneels to place a hand on my back.

I don't know what to do. Let alone what to say.

I walk to the car and pull Carol's suitcase out.

"I need a favor." Eric opens the passenger door of his truck, and I jump in. Jay helps me with the suitcase and jumps in the back. "Wherever you want to go," he says.

"I need you to drive me to the San Francisco Airport,"

And on the highway, I put the window down. I let the air run through my hair, and I don't feel like talking. I don't feel anything.

A void is forming where love once was, and I feel nothing anymore. I think of Jack for a moment and my heart hurts, so I focus on covering the pain with something else.

I feel used.

I feel embarrassed.

Primarily disappointed at Carol.

We were taught to be good, to be women of respect and consideration. I keep hoping that Carol didn't know what she was doing. My mind puzzles me to think that my sister had something to do with the death of children, children that belonged to the man I loved.

And on the other side, I am unhappy for her. Hating that she tried and failed. My heart hurts for many reasons.

I feel like a shadow without its owner. Like I'm walking alongside of a desert scattered with dead bodies. Like I am next.

I inhale deeply because I can't breathe properly.

I lost everything. I lost my parents. I lost my sister and my aunt. And I lost Jack! I thought we were going to spend more time together.

And then the what-ifs: If I just stayed home that day, nothing would have happened.

This is my fault.

Carol, why?

Why did you do this?

I want to go back and tell Jack that I am sorry. I want to beg for forgiveness and ask him to let me in once again. I want to be there again.

I look at Eric, and he is focused on driving. There is no sound, just the sound of the wind rushing by. I wipe my face, and Eric places his hand on my thigh, and I look at him. He smiles, and I look outside again.

I don't even have anything to say to him, other than a thank you. I would be dead if it weren't for him.

We arrive at night time. I sit up straight and look outside in disbelief. I ask Eric why everyone is out and why people walk around like nothing happened. This city is vibrant. People are out shopping and eating at restaurants without care.

"Big cities aren't like Stockton or Modesto," he says.

"You mean my family and I were locked up for nothing,"

"I wouldn't say nothing. It would have been better if you guys moved to a big city,"

Staring at open restaurants, I bite my tongue. It was all fake. It was all for nothing. Carol and Aunt Megan died for nothing! We lived in fear when we could have been living here! If we just had stayed put in San Francisco when my grandpa was alive, nothing would have ever happened.

Another hole inside my chest. I bite my tongue and my chest rumbles. This is stupid.

But why get angry now. It's all over.

I hear a rumbling, and I look towards a large airplane pulling up into the sky. I see a massive building, several people walking in and out from it. Eric parks and walks out with me. He pulls me in for a hug, and I hold him tighter.

He lifts himself and cleans a tear off my face.

"It's better this way,"

"I know,"

He pulls out a little piece of paper from his pocket. "I'm sorry about your sister," I hug him again and rest my head on his chest. "Can I ask you something?" He lifts and waits for me to ask. "Did Carol know what she was doing?"

"I don't know...."

Eric hands me money and the piece of paper, "What is this?" I ask. "Jack gave it to me this morning and told me to give it to you,"

"For me?"

"Yeah,"

I stare at the paper without looking at it and place it inside Carol's bag. Jay jumps out and hugs me. "Good luck, Kate," he says. "Thank you, guys," Eric smiles. And a few moments later, I hear the truck drive away.

And here I am.

Everything I wanted, gone. All I wanted right now was to be with Jack. For him to hug me, wrap his hands around me and kiss me.

But no.

Today was it; my impromptu farewell.

CHAPTER 56

I put the money inside the backpack and face the airport.

I don't have time to feel anything. From this moment on, I must force myself not to feel a thing. My heart turns hollow, and I need to carry on. Don't bother; the void is going to be filled somehow.

Just the thought of Jack broke me, so I shake my head every time I think of him. No more. Not anymore.

I see a sign over a counter that says, "Europe Airlines." And I walk to it. "Hi, how can I help you dear," A lady says behind the counter.

"I would like a plane to Europe, please,"

She smiles and gives me a confused look. "Where in Europe?" She asks. Reaching inside the backpack, I feel the paper that Jack gave me, and I pull to read it:

Kate's Parents: Andrew and Cristina Preston

Location: American Refugee Camp of Liverpool, England

I choke and I bite my lip to hold myself from crying. He found them for me.

He did it! I can't believe it.

I fold the paper and put it in my pocket as I lift my head, "Liverpool, England." I say.

"Oh, I hear Liverpool is beautiful this time of year,"

She hands me a long piece of paper and points in a direction. And as I walk up, I sit beside the bench. I start to cry as I stare at the ticket. And I think of our last moment together. "Stop," I whisper.

But it hurts.

It hurts not having him near me.

I didn't mean to hurt him. I didn't …

A man calls my number and a lady dressed in blue directs me to my seat. Another lady comes by and asks me for my ticket. She holds it, stamps it, and hands it back to me. I look at it and see a symbol stamped on top—this stamp of a blue feather encircled by a gold ring.

"Thank you for flying with Europe Airlines" the speaker announces. And as I toy with the ticket, I stare at the blue feather. A beautiful feather, a bird's feather.

I lay my head back, and all I can hear is Aunt Megan's voice:

"When things get cold, birds fly away to where it is safe,"

And things got cold. Really cold.

"And when things get warm again, birds fly back to their home, back to their safe haven, and to where they love the most."

Oh, how I envy the birds.

That's where Aunt Megan was wrong. Some things do not get better. Some things do not get warm anymore. That's where she failed. That's where Carol failed. Some things are better left cold and un-touched.

And that's the saddest part.

Where was my haven?

My haven was with Jack.

But it isn't safe anymore. I know that with Jack, things will never get back to normal. Things will nev-er be "warm" once again. He is gone.

I will never see him anymore. Never kiss him. Never hug him. Never once say "I love you" again. I will be leaving for good and that makes me miserable.

But I love him.

No. Stop.

I know that there is no possible way that he would ever accept me anymore. Not this way, not after this. Even if I explained myself a thousand times, things cannot be ok anymore.

Birds have mastered their way back home.

They know when to return, what trees to come to, what mountains to stop at and when it is safe again.

My home is gone.

My city is broken.

My family disappeared.

Carol is gone, and I've lost Jack forever.

I don't have that choice. I am not a bird.

Even if I return someday, I will never be able to go back home and see my city, let alone face Jack.

And it feels horrible knowing I will never have Jack back. And that is why I envy the birds.